"Haven't you learned yet, Larissa?" Alessandro spoke so forcefully the ghost of old Venice whispered through the polished patina of his perfect English. 'In some matters it is of no use to be *wise*."

He pounded the table with his fist, making the silver jump. "There are moments in your life that you need to seize with both your hands."

Lara stared at him in shock, her heart thudding at some veiled comprehension she couldn't quite read. "Well—well, how do I know this is one of them?"

He touched his linen napkin to his lips, then threw it down and sprang to his feet. Before she even had time to react he seized her and dragged her up out of her chair, thundering, "This is *how*."

Even if at times work is rather boring,
there is one person making the office a whole
lot more interesting: the boss!

Dark and dangerous, alpha and powerful,
rich and ruthless… He's in control, he knows
what he wants and he's going to get it!
He's tall, handsome and breathtakingly attractive.
And there's one outcome that's never in doubt—
the heroines of these supersexy
stories will be:

From sensible suits…into satin sheets!

A sexy miniseries available only from
Harlequin Presents®!

Anna Cleary

AT THE BOSS'S BECK AND CALL

Undressed
BY THE BOSS

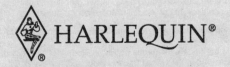

HARLEQUIN®

TORONTO • NEW YORK • LONDON
AMSTERDAM • PARIS • SYDNEY • HAMBURG
STOCKHOLM • ATHENS • TOKYO • MILAN • MADRID
PRAGUE • WARSAW • BUDAPEST • AUCKLAND

Recycling programs
for this product may
not exist in your area.

ISBN-13: 978-0-373-12882-2

AT THE BOSS'S BECK AND CALL

First North American Publication 2009.

www.eHarlequin.com

Printed in U.S.A.

All about the author...
Anna Cleary

As a child, **ANNA CLEARY** loved reading so much that during the midnight hours she was forced to read with a torch under the bedcovers, to lull the suspicions of her sleep-obsessed parents. From an early age she dreamed of writing her own books. She saw herself in a stone cottage by the sea, wearing a velvet smoking jacket and sipping sherry, like Somerset Maugham.

In real life she became a schoolteacher, and her greatest pleasure was teaching children to write beautiful stories.

A little while ago, she and one of her friends made a pact to each write the first chapter of a romance novel during their holidays. From writing her very first line, Anna was hooked, and she gave up teaching to become a full-time writer. She now lives in Queensland, Australia, with a deeply sensitive and intelligent cat. She prefers champagne to sherry, and loves music, books, four-legged people, trees, movies and restaurants.

For Sally, my inspiration

CHAPTER ONE

ONLY a few minutes late. No need to panic.

Alighting from an overheated bus into bustling George Street on a Sydney winter morn, waiting, shivering, at the crossing lights in her little charcoal suit and her suede knee boots, making the dash with the crowd across to the opposite pavement, Lara Meadows reminded herself she was strong.

She was brave, she was still beautiful—well, in an artistic sense. From a distance. If she dived into a fountain in her underwear she could come out looking as shapely as any goddess of the silver screen, if more generously covered than some. Though only where it *counted*. If her hair got wet it would go limp and lose the pale spun silk effect she still managed to achieve to confound her critics, but she could still look reasonable.

Her hand flew to the scar at the base of her nape.

Not that she was competitive, by any means, or that looks meant anything in the publishing world. No, it was far more important that she was smart and professional, she was good at her job, she could speak up for herself...

So why were her insides churning like a cement mixer?

Alessandro was only a man, after all. Six years ago he hadn't been formidable. He'd been the ultimate in amusing, sophisticated and charming. Take him apart bit by bit— remove his thick black hair, his smiling dark eyes, his sensuous mouth, his voice, his long powerful limbs, his *chest*…and what would he be left with to make her knees knock together? She had done nothing to be ashamed of. He was the one who should be worried.

She pushed through the glass doors of the Stiletto building and sprinted across to the lift. No one else from her floor was around. They'd all be upstairs in the meeting room, eager to con the big bosses from across the globe into believing they were always punctual.

Eager to impress Alessandro.

She gulped in a breath. She'd *meant* to be early, but plaits took time, and Vivi liked them just right. Then there was the walk to school—it just didn't seem fair to rush a five-year-old fascinated by every living creature along the way.

She reminded herself of how tolerant and easy-going Alessandro was. Surely he was the last person anyone needed to fear as a boss.

Unless… She experienced a definite stab of fear. Unless it was someone who hadn't yet managed to inform him of something he might think concerned him quite dramatically.

Alessandro Vincenti accepted a file from the quavering secretary with grave thanks. The woman, bequeathed to him by the failed Managing Director of Stiletto Publishing, and possibly anxious about her future, backed towards the door, poised to scurry to safety. Alessandro sent her a reassuring smile. It had never been his pleasure to intimidate gentle creatures. Let the waters of the pond of life remain clear and unruffled.

With his habitual ease he tilted back in the leather chair and opened the folder. Australians could be an interesting people, he remembered, if a little bizarre. A nation that idolised bush-rangers and ridiculed its politicians was not as uncomplicated as it might appear on the surface. What was the affectionate term they used to describe their rebels? Larrikin, that was it. They smiled at their larrikins.

In an effort to familiarise himself with the staff, on paper at least, before he soothed them with his motivational spiel, he leafed through the sparse array of pages pertaining to the various departments, if they could be called that. *Dio*, had anyone ever checked the record-keeping in this place? What had the MD been doing before his meltdown?

He took a moment to peruse the personnel list.

Curious, the poetry contained within names.

Halfway through the editorial section, his gaze arrested and locked to *one* name. A name that sprang from the page and clicked on a part of him he'd long since believed inert. A name redolent of drowsy afternoons on sun-drenched beaches, blonde silken hair and the scent of summer grass. His blood quickened to the recollection of a dusk, fragrant with honeysuckle and the promise of love.

Could it be…? Could it really be…?

'Er…Beryl.' He glanced up at the secretary, arresting her doorwards creep and causing her to jump. 'This L. Meadows now—who is he?' He held the page a little away from him between long, fastidious fingers.

The secretary's words fell over each other in her haste to please. '*She*. She's a she. I mean a—a *woman*, Mr Vincenti. Lara Meadows. She's been with Stiletto now for about six months. Bill—I mean Mr Carmichael, our MD, I mean ex-MD, liked her very much.'

A long-dormant visceral nerve made a raw pinch in Alessandro's gut.

So. *She* was still in the world.

For the benefit of the secretary he allowed no facial muscle to register his shock, pretending interest in other names on the list of Scala Enterprises' most recently acquired workforce.

'And who is this?' he continued smoothly down the list, as though Lara Meadows had never made a fool of him. Never caused him to feel—whatever it had been. Never brought him to his emotional knees like some love-crazed Don José bellowing from the opera stage about his Carmen. 'And this one? Tell me about him.'

Amazing, to find Lara after all this time. What were the odds she'd be working for the very company they'd settled on as their foothold in the southern hemisphere? He narrowed his eyes. If this were the same Lara. His *Larissa*.

The nerve twisted. Though surely she'd be married by now, unless she'd kept her maiden name after her marriage?

To some poor fool, some sucker who didn't mind being let down.

And of course Bill would have liked her very much. It was probably *liking* her that had brought the guy to his ruin. He glanced at the secretary's eager face, weighing up whether to hazard a question, then discarded the notion. It was exactly what the woman was longing for. Any tiny morsel, no matter how trivial, to whisper about the visiting boss to the staff.

And he felt no interest in Lara Meadows. That moment in time when her capricious whims, her irrational Hollywood-inspired *tests* had burned deep into his essential being was past. A woman incapable of valuing the sincerity of an honest man was below the radar of his consciousness.

Still, he wouldn't be human if he couldn't appreciate the irony in the situation. Whether she'd known it or not, Ms Meadows had once held his fate in her hands. Now, he held her livelihood in his. If he were one of those mediaeval Vincentis given to vendettas…

Revenge, a dish best served cold, had often been his mother's dry observation. Were six years long enough to cool a blaze that had consumed him and reduced his dignity to ashes? Or so he'd thought at the time.

Alessandro shrugged, amused at his momentary regression to youthful passion. On second thoughts, it would be interesting to see her again. See how she would look.

How she would face him.

* * *

Anyway, Lara reflected, scanning her face in the lift mirror, by this time he could be bald, or morbidly paunched. Her memories of him might have been distorted by time.

On the approach to the conference room, though, her legs grew wobbly and reluctant with dread. But face it. Despite everything, she was excited. The thought of seeing him again was rushing through her like a summer storm.

Although, could she really expect Alessandro to remember her with the same intensity as she remembered him? With what she knew about him now, he might not remember her at all. Six years was a long time for an international playboy to hold an idea.

She paused outside and made an effort to calm her breathing, but ever since the news had broken the old video show in her head wouldn't stop spinning through the reels.

Six years ago. Her first and only international book conference. The publishing company she'd been with at the time wouldn't have been able to afford to send her if it hadn't been held here in Sydney. It had been her first conference. Her first...

Everything.

That initial, fantastic connection at the cocktail party. The amused glance he'd exchanged with her over the ridiculous sci-fi diva with the hair. The strawberry daiquiri he'd wangled for her. He'd screwed up his handsome face at her choice but she'd pretended to enjoy it. Then the charmed days that had followed. The long walks. The intense conversations about literature, music, Shakespeare—everything she was most passionate about.

Alessandro refused to describe himself as Italian, or Venetian. He was a citizen of the world, he'd told her with a laugh, yet he'd treated her ideas with such respect, as if they were as clever and original as his own. She'd never been so riveted by conversation with anyone. So excited, so—enchanted. Every word he'd uttered had held her on the most delicious hook.

And when she'd found out the origin of his family name...

She'd looked it up on the internet. No wonder she'd been starry-eyed. He'd been reluctant to answer her bombardment of questions at first, but he'd finally relented and told her a little about his branch of the Venetian Vincentis. His fore-fathers had been marquises since the earliest days of the Venetian Republic. Those early marquises had been among the noble families responsible for electing each Doge as head of the country, and had served on the Council that had assisted the Doge to govern Venice.

All the way back to the earliest records each of Alessandro's forefathers had been designated Marchese d'Isole Veneziane Minori, which meant Marquis of the Minor Venetian Isles. So beautiful. So *romantic*.

He'd winced when she brought it up, but when she'd grilled him over it Alessandro had eventually admitted that in terms of family inheritance, he was the current *marchese*.

The Marchese d'Isole Veneziane Minori. After a bit of practice, the words had just rolled off her tongue. Marquis of the Minor Venetian Isles.

Oh, God, she'd been so impressed. She'd mocked him about it, teased him, but she'd been so utterly ravished Alessandro had laughed at her. It had been on that first golden afternoon at the beach.

She closed her eyes now to think of him stretched beside her, his lean, tanned body still glistening from the surf, his black hair gleaming, those deep, dark eyes, so sensual, so intent on her and her alone. That was when he'd kissed her for the first time. Afterwards, they'd had dinner, and then after *that*…

Even now, any mention of the Seasons hotel gave her a pang. If the walls of that suite had been able to talk…

His week had turned into two, then three, then stretched on through the summer until he could no longer put off going back for the start of his final semester at the Harvard Business School, where his firm was sending him. Her last glimpse of him before he boarded the plane had been so blurred with her tears she'd knocked over a small elderly woman, but the promise had kept her afloat.

The pact.

As always when she thought of it her stomach gave a churn. She'd have kept her side of it if she could, if only Fate hadn't got in the way. Like a trusting fool, she'd have been there to meet him, just in case he *had* decided to come back. But there'd been the bushfires, her father, then her dreadful time in hospital. And afterwards…

Oh, God. Afterwards, a seismic shift in who and what she was.

But Alessandro didn't *know* that. If she could just hang onto that fact…

She steeled her nerve, and gave the conference-room door a gentle inwards push.

The small room seemed crammed. Not that Stiletto had such a large staff, only six in editorial, plus two part-time assistants, but it was rare to see everyone assembled at the same time. With the publicity staff, and the sales and production people, the numbers swelled to the twenties. Grateful to see an empty chair not too far inside the door, Lara crept to it as noiselessly as she could.

All the organised people who'd managed to arrive on time were sitting silent and watchful, listening. In the absence of Bill, their dreamy, slightly slipshod ex-Managing Director, Cinta from Sales and Marketing had volunteered to stand up on behalf of the company. Looking as sinuous as ever in a dress that had been spray-painted to her bones, Cinta was delivering a flowery welcome speech for the takeover team in the sultry voice she assumed for really attractive men.

Alessandro.

Lara spotted him at once, her heart shaking like a quake zone. A glimpse only, a mere flash, but it was him all right, seated to one side of the lectern, right next to the terrifyingly groomed woman with the razor cut bob and the fantastic suit whom Cinta introduced as Donatuila Capelli, one of Scala's top executives from the New York office. Lara could believe it. Every thread the woman wore screamed Fifth Avenue.

Lara sat down just as Donatuila got up to deliver a few bracing words in a fabulous deep, husky Manhattan accent, before embarking on a slick presentation of the latest on Scala's product sales. Lara was thankful that, with so much going on, Alessandro wouldn't have noticed her late arrival. She was so glad she'd decided to dress up, even if her boots were killers.

At the other end of the room, Alessandro sat frozen for seconds, then deliberately relaxed his muscles and concentrated on breathing until the roaring sensation in his blood eased. It was *her*. No doubt of it, that late arrival was Lara Meadows. The blonde hair he remembered, if quite a lot longer now, the distinctive tilt of her chin, her graceful, willowy form. No other woman entering a room had ever had that effect on him.

And neither would she, ever again. It had simply been the shock of the initial sighting. Understandable, considering he'd scanned the room and resigned himself to believing her absent. It had even occurred to him that she might have quit rather than face him. But no, she wasn't lying low or fleeing for cover. Unlike the rest of her colleagues, she was merely late.

Late.

He had to hand it to her. That behaviour was nothing short of casual.

He made an infinitesimal lean to the right, and in a chink between the rows saw her cross her legs as she relaxed into her chair. The long, shapely legs he remembered were partially encased in long boots, drawing attention to silky, smooth knees. Sexy, but... Something like a hot needle pierced his professional composure and homed straight to that raw nerve. *Insolente* was the word that boiled up in him.

The sheer gall of her to be late. The gall. Of all the people

in the room who should be anxious to demonstrate courtesy…
Who should have left no stone unturned to ensure of meeting
her obligation this morning.

Here was a woman who knew nothing of respect.

If Lara craned her neck she could just see one lean hand
resting on a dark-clad knee. A further tilt and she could see
his face. A study in bronze and ebony, he was frowning down
at the floor, his black brows lowered, but even from this
distance she could see he had the same thick, dark lashes, the
classically sculpted cheekbones and chiselled jaw.

That handsome jaw was sternly set, in fact, making him
look rather grimmer than she'd hoped, until something
Donatuila Capelli said roused him from his reverie and he
lifted his gaze to her with a polite, questioning smile.

Then the most ravishing thing about that lean, strong face
came flooding back to Lara with such evocative power every
muscle in her body made an involuntary clench.

That devil's mockery in the tilt of his brows. The ability of
his firm, sensuous mouth to remain grave, even solemn, when
he was amused. And his eyes. Those brilliant dark eyes, so
seductive, so expressive of fathomless depths of subtlety and
sophistication.

Ignoring her mad pulse, Lara clung to her chair and held
herself taut and resistant. She was over him. She'd been over
him long since. He was the man who'd kissed her goodbye,
then married someone else. But when he uncoiled his long,
lean limbs with leisurely grace, rose, swept them all with a
long, deep glance, then commenced his address in his beautiful, deep, faintly accented voice, she remembered why she'd
gone overboard.

Fallen in love.

Gone truly, madly, deeply…*insane*.

She shrank into her chair, her heart racketing into a drum-
roll. Had he seen her yet?

Alessandro sent a measuring glance over the small audience in their jeans and boots and arty jewellery, careful to avoid the back row and the blonde whose imprint was branded onto his soul.

Normally, he was a tolerant administrator. When Head Office sent him out after a takeover to settle the blood and dust, then restructure the new acquisition into an entity resembling a company, it was his practice to reassure the new workforce of their job security, offer them a pay-rise and improve their conditions.

Unfortunately, there were some situations when a man needed to make his authority clear and unequivocal. This irreverent attitude some Australians had, this *casualness*, needed to be checked. The arrogance displayed by some employees of this sad little company needed to be nipped in the bud. Let them quake a little while he showed them how tenuous their comfort zones really were.

There would be no larrikins working for Scala Enterprises.

Discarding the soothing tone it was his practice to open with, he postponed mention of the gifts he'd come bearing, and cut directly to business.

'Prepare yourselves for some changes.'

At first Lara hardly heard the words that held her colleagues pinned to their chairs, delivered in Alessandro's dark *cioccolata* tones. There was an electric tension in the room outside her own, but she was too absorbed in examining her ex-lover, drinking in every detail of him, to register immediately the full import of everything he said.

As she gazed at his beautiful, austere face a wave of poignant emotion welled up in her and she could barely hold back tears. So much was associated with him in her heart.

If this cool, authoritarian Alessandro wasn't quite the man who'd flirted with and teased her and made her feel like the most desirable woman in the world, he was sexier, if possible. Still so lithe and athletic-looking in his dark, exquisitely cut suit, with his olive tan and five-o'clock shadow, it was clear he took rigorous care of that powerful six-three frame. She calculated that he must be nearly thirty-five, since she'd just turned twenty-seven. An experienced, man-of-the-world thirty-five. In six years the character lines in his lean, handsome face had deepened, and he looked more focused, the image of a successful, hard-headed businessman.

And a *marchese*.

One whose dulcet tones could point out some harsh realities. She stopped listening for that elusive accent, and started hearing the words. Apart from that paper he'd delivered at the book convention, she'd never really seen him before in his professional role. Who'd have imagined he'd be so autocratic? It was easy to believe he was a *marchese*. With his dark eyes so stern, even Cinta's smile was beginning to develop a fixed plasticity.

As the words achieved more traction the alarm in the room became almost tangible. Lara noticed even the self-possessed Donatuila shoot him a couple of narrow glances.

'You have failed as a company,' he accused, steel in his deep, cool voice, 'and I fully intend to rescue you, however painful that might be. At the end of next week Ms Capelli and I will be attending the International Book Convention in Bangkok as delegates. Before we leave, we will have finalised the new management and restructured Stiletto Publishing. You will be on the path to transforming from a small isolated company to being a vibrant part of a global organisation. Of course, you will all require some re-education. Some of you will find it necessary to invest your free time.'

There was an uneasy shuffling among the staff, but he continued on with inexorable calm. 'Every publishing project, every job in every department will come under the microscope. And in return…' He softened his tone, and not a muscle moved as the room held its breath. There was something so chilling in the pleasant cadences of his voice, with every consonant, every sibilant, so clear and distinct.

'From those of you who keep your jobs I demand dedication. All employees of Scala Enterprises are expected to deliver a one-hundred-per-cent performance. This applies to the large things, as well as to the small. From achieving your project goals, to meeting your deadlines, to the scrupulous observance of punctuality. And I mean punctuality in all things. Your arrival at work, your return from your breaks, your attendance at meetings.'

Guilt jolted through Lara and she sank back into her chair as his unforgiving gaze roved from face to face. She felt the heat of it sear hers without noticing any change in his expression. No softening of recognition. It was as though he didn't *want* to see her.

He added with lethal softness, 'I think I should warn you, it is a very rare excuse I find myself able to accept.'

Her heart sank. The magic of a dew-spangled spider's web hanging above the schoolyard fence hardly seemed likely to rate.

'When you know me better,' he continued smoothly, 'you will discover that I do not like to be kept waiting. At Scala, there is no room for human frailty. We are uncompromising in regard to people meeting their obligations.' He wound up with the grim warning, 'Over the next couple of days Ms Capelli and I will be meeting with each and every one of you. Be prepared to defend your right to your job.'

A ripple of shock reverberated through the staff. Then, exactly as though his address had been a cosy chat, with polished courtesy Alessandro Vincenti thanked them all for their attention and dismissed them.

Lara rose with everyone else and joined the exodus from the room, but once beside her desk she halted. Shouldn't she speak to him at once? Break the ice?

She shouldered her way back through the end stragglers and into the conference room, but Alessandro and his associate had already left, no doubt in a hurry to start the bloodletting. She hesitated a second. Would it be wise to interrupt him at this point? He seemed so efficient and remote, this might not be the best time to revive their old acquaintance. Although, it might be an advantage to at least inform him of her presence. The last thing she wanted was to give him the impression she had anything to be nervous about.

With that in mind she hurried along the corridor to Bill's old office, her pulse pumping as fast as if she'd been a bad girl summoned to the headmaster.

The door was closed, probably for the first time in its history. She stood there a few seconds, breathing carefully to centre herself. She was brave, she was strong, she was a mother. She could deal with Alessandro Vincenti, woman to man, though she couldn't help wondering if he'd still find her attractive.

Ignoring her galloping heartbeat, she raised her fist and knocked. She was just about to try again when Donatuila Capelli swept around the corner and, spotting her there, strode up on her four-inch stilettos.

Attractive in a corporate-Morticia-Addams kind of way, she delivered Lara a cool, sharp scrutiny from her long, cleverly made-up brown eyes. 'Do you want something?'

'I—came to see Alessandro.'

'Mr Vincenti to you, honey. What's your name?'

'Lara.' She indicated the door. 'Is he…?'

Donatuila raised her thinly pencilled eyebrows. 'No, he's not. And I suggest you go back to your desk and wait your turn.' She grasped the door handle and practically edged Lara aside with her bony hip. 'You'll get your chance with him, same as everyone else.'

Donatuila opened the door and went in.

The door closed in Lara's face, and she felt some indignation. Whew. What a cold burr. Donatuila Capelli was brisk. It made her wonder if she'd been wise to draw attention to herself. Perhaps it had been a mistake to attempt to talk to Alessandro privately.

She was about to turn away when the door opened again.

Alessandro's tall frame filled the doorway, his dark eyes clashing with hers while the stars arrested in their orbits and hung suspended in space for breathless seconds.

Her senses burst open in a weakening rush like flowers to the sun. She'd forgotten how he smelled. Soap, leather shoes, aftershave, clothes freshly laundered in some lemony agent. And, beneath all that, some barely detectable scent to do with raw masculinity and sophistication that evoked all the old sensations. The thrill in her heart. The longing.

His deep, dark eyes made a slow flicker over her, then settled on her face.

'Oh, Alessandro,' she breathed. 'I just thought I'd say—hello.'

Something flashed in the depths of his eyes, then his stirringly expressive mouth hardened the merest fraction. After a second he moved politely aside and motioned her in.

Another desk had been crammed in beside Bill's big executive piece. Donatuila Capelli was seated there, studying a thick, ring-bound folder. Alessandro nodded at her and held the door wide.

'Tuila, please excuse us. This will take less than a second.'

Donatuila's head jerked up and she made a faint, incredulous *tsk* with her tongue, then put down the folder, rose and crossed to the door, casting Lara a blistering look that Lara felt rather than saw, overwhelmed as she was by the presence of her lover. *Ex*-lover, she reminded herself.

Alessandro closed the door, and Lara was alone with him. Again.

She'd forgotten how intensely magnetic he was. It went deeper than his brilliant dark eyes and hard masculine beauty. Something in him pulled her at a deep, visceral level that made her want to press her body into his lean, powerful frame and hold him to her with all her might.

For goodness sake, her brain tried to bellow, the man was married. *Kill* that thought.

It was her body that didn't understand. Her senses, and her

instincts. Her affections, and her primal feminine responses to the raw, primitive male beneath the crisp, elegant clothes. Of course she knew she couldn't expect him to kiss her, after so long, and with a wife and all, but every one of her skin cells tingled with a yearning to walk straight into his arms.

As though he was unaware of her internal confusion, his manner was cool and courteous. Like that of a top executive. Or a *marchese* who knew his minions would jump to his command without him ever having to raise his voice.

'Yes?' he asked, scouring her face with a dark, searching gaze. 'Is there something you need?'

She felt a pang of anxiety, and made an involuntary move to touch him. To her dismay, he moved his hand away. Discreetly, but nonetheless firmly.

Her throat dried. 'You—you do remember me, don't you? *Lara…*?'

His eyes glinted and it took him a moment to reply. Then he said, 'Vaguely. The Sydney International Book Convention, wasn't it?' His cool, inscrutable gaze lasered into hers, then he lowered his black lashes and, with a sardonic twitch of his brows, glanced at his watch. 'Can I help you? Is there something in particular?'

Stunned, she stared at him for a moment, then shook her head. 'Well, no. I only wanted to…say hi.'

His brows drew together and he let out a faint, exasperated breath. 'I don't really have time for reminiscing. I'm sure you understand—we are on a tight schedule. So…unless there's something specific?'

Cold shock slammed through her, but pride and the automatic social response held her together.

'Well, no, no, nothing specific,' she said, flushing, her pulse pounding in her ears. 'Nothing all that worth mentioning, in fact. I'm—so sorry to have interrupted your work.'

She swept from the room with a cool, proud smile, though

her eyes, like her sensibilities, were smarting. She'd never felt more of a fool.

She went to the Ladies and sat in a cubicle for a few minutes, her hot face in her trembling hands until her cheeks cooled a little, while her brain seethed with some of the specific things she could have said. Things like… *What took you so long?* Or… *Hi, Dad. There's someone I want you to meet.*

In the office he'd commandeered, Alessandro strolled to the desk and picked up a page of candidates that had already been shortlisted for the managing director's position. He stared at it, unseeing, for seconds, a rapid thumping in his chest.

The nerve of her, to sashay up to his office and claim him as a friend. She'd deserved that rebuff, but why did she have to look so…?

His gut clenched. She was just another blonde. The world abounded in pretty blondes. If only…

If only he hadn't seen into her eyes.

He dropped the crushed list of candidates just as the phone rang. He wasn't a violent man, but he raised his hand to sweep the phone off the desk. Restraining himself just in time, he lifted the receiver and dropped it gently back onto its cradle.

Sacramento. She deserved everything he gave her. Everything.

CHAPTER TWO

IN LARA'S office, people were venting their feelings.

'No room for human frailty! Did you hear that? What a crock.'

'Did you see his eyes? How can anyone be so hot and icy cold at the same time?'

'Hot, cruel and ruthless. You only have to look at his mouth. Oh-h-h…' Lara's neighbour closed her eyes and breathed '…that mouth.'

Lara sat silent at her desk while the comments washed around her, trying to come to terms with this other Alessandro, this cold, efficient Alessandro who felt nothing for her now, not even friendship. How could a snub be so polite and feel so savage at the same time? Regardless though, she still couldn't help feeling ridiculously sensitive to everything they said about him.

Kirsten, their senior, took a relaxed view. 'I suppose we could have expected something like this. Scala isn't exactly a charity. With them it's about the bottom line. We might even enjoy a little bit of organisation around here. And I guess we can all defend our own corners, can't we?' She winked. 'Anyway, *that* guy won't want to be hanging about in this outpost of civilisation for long, so he won't waste time appointing the new MD. He won't even be here long enough to discover our charms before he'll be gone like *that*.' She clicked her fingers.

Lara tried to keep her face from revealing anything. What would they say if they knew he'd already discovered hers? That suite at the Seasons had been enshrined in her heart as one of the sacred spots in Sydney.

She'd never forget their last afternoon.

Before Alessandro, she'd never been in a really expensive hotel. He'd commandeered a suite for his stay, with a little sitting room opening from the bedroom. The windows were wide, with spectacular views of the harbour and the Opera House.

She'd dreaded that last day's dawning with every fibre of her being. It had been their most beautiful, and the hardest. Every second had been precious, every moment bittersweet, with goodbye looming over them like Armageddon.

She'd done her best to conceal her heartache. Alessandro had teased her about being quiet at first, then had himself become unusually quiet and grave. After lunch he'd taken her up to his room. To mull things over, he'd said.

He'd poured the champagne. Clinked glasses with her. Toasted her.

Before she'd even had time to sip hers, he'd gently taken the glass from her hand and set it down, then, with his dark eyes so fierce and intense that she'd actually trembled with excitement, he'd swiftly and expertly stripped off her clothes and flattened her to the bed.

And it had been fantastic. So heartfelt and emotional. It must have been one of their most impassioned feats of lovemaking.

Afterwards, lying beside him, tracing the lean, hard contours of his bronzed body with her fingers, she'd winched up all her courage.

She'd begun, as casually as possible, 'You know, Alessandro, I'll—miss you.' She'd given a small laugh, for fear he'd guess the frightening force of her feelings. 'I really do wish—you weren't going.'

There'd been a tiny tremor in her voice. Had she gone too far?

He'd been silent for such an eternity, his elbow crooked

over his eyes while her heart trembled in terror. Just when she'd been ready to hit the self-destruct button, his voice had come from so deep within him it had been like a groan.

'I *have* to go.' Then he'd turned on his side towards her. It had been an electric moment. Instead of their usual cool amusement, his dark eyes were glowing, their gaze warm and compelling.

'So, *tesoro*. I've been thinking too. Why don't you come?'

She'd stared at him in shock. 'What? You mean…to America?'

'Sure, America. Why not? You'll love it. It's only for a few months. When the semester finishes I go back to *Italia*.' Then he'd added lightly, as if dropping the words into a pool to see what ripples formed, 'You can come home with me.'

Home. When she didn't answer at once, too many wild pictures flashing through her head—her job, her parents, plunging into the unknown with him when she hardly knew him. *Overseas*, when she'd hardly even been out of New South Wales.

Venice.

The Marquis of the Minor Venetian Isles. So thrilling. So—scary.

He'd added, 'We would be—a couple.'

This was *it*, she'd thought in the first wild lurching moments of shooting stars and ecstasy. Unbelievably, she'd found her man, and such a beautiful, fantastic man. A cultured, civilised, gentle man. A man she could talk to. A man with whom she could share the secrets of her soul.

But, some rational part of her had squeaked, how much of a commitment was he actually offering? How well did she know him, really?

What did couple mean? Lovers? *Partners?*

And what about her job? Her family?

'Wow,' she'd said, scrabbling for the words while her brain reeled from the possibilities like a woman with vertigo on the roof edge of a fifty-storey tower block. 'That would be—fantastic. I'm—overwhelmed, honestly, Alessandro. Honoured.' Perhaps some part of her uncertainty had shown on her face, because he'd made a small grimace.

'Honoured,' he'd echoed, lilting his brows in some bemusement. Then she'd seen a flicker in his eyes she hadn't seen there before, and it wrung her heart to think she might have hurt him.

He'd said very quietly, such gentle dignity in his deep, masculine tones, 'Is this your way of saying no, *tesoro*?'

'No, no,' she'd hastened to reassure him. 'Not at all. It's just that… Well, you know it's so—so sudden…I might just need a minute to draw breath.' She'd beamed at him, though her heart was pounding like mad, and everything in her was screaming to her to slam on the brakes. 'Wait, though, hang on. I've had a thought. I don't have a passport.'

She'd been so relieved to have that perfectly good reason to put forward, but he'd frowned and shaken his head, as if, in the civilised world he came from, minor obstacles like that could be brushed away.

'I can change my flight again,' he said. 'Added to all the others, what's another day? Twenty-four hours should be long enough for us to organise your passport.'

There'd been a further desperate moment while the offer still hung in the balance, and that was when she'd had the inspiration of the pact. The love test.

'All right. No, wait, look, I know. I have an idea— Alessandro, darling…' She'd never dared call him that before, and she could see it registered with him. It had given her the courage to go on. 'It's all been so fast. Maybe—maybe we should give ourselves a chance to be certain we're doing the right thing.'

For a second his thick black lashes had swept down to screen his eyes. 'You're not sure you want to be with me?'

She'd drawn a sharp breath, then said quickly, 'I do. Of

course I do. But I'd just like some time to get organised. You know, I'll have to say goodbye to Mum and Dad—and give notice at work. And you might need to think about it too. If we—just give ourselves a little bit of time to think. We could do something like they did in that movie. Did you ever see *An Affair to Remember* with Cary Grant and Deborah Kerr?'

He hadn't seen the old movie classic, and, in truth, he hadn't been so keen on her idea of delaying a few weeks. He'd gone rather scarily still and inscrutable, like a *marchese* whose pride had taken a hit. As if she should have been able to make up her mind to go with him on the spot. As if she should have just left her life behind her, not taken a moment to think and give her parents a chance to get used to the idea, to weigh up all the pros and cons.

He had agreed at last, although with reservations.

She'd been so young, she'd truly believed it was the right thing to do. The *wise* thing. Alessandro had swept her along with him on a giddy, emotional ride and she'd barely had time to snatch a breath. And while the top of the Centrepoint Tower in Sydney didn't have quite the same romantic cachet as the Empire State building in New York, if he *had* met her there again in six weeks' time, to her it would have been close enough to heaven.

Sadly, as it had turned out, her instinct had been the right one.

Even if she had been able to make it to the Centrepoint Tower at four p.m. that fateful Wednesday, Alessandro wouldn't have met her there. She knew now that he wouldn't, because all the time he'd been wining and dining and seducing her in Sydney, his fiancée had been back home in Italy preparing for the wedding.

She'd found that all out later. And when she'd discovered the devastating truth, she'd come to the miserable realisation that, like the practised seduction artist he was, he'd probably pretended to agree to the pact so he could leave her on an up-note.

Occasionally, though rarely now, she'd suffered a cold twinge of fear that he might actually have flown all the way back from Harvard Business School only to find that she'd failed to show up, but she always rationalised that worry away. Of course he wouldn't have. His mid-semester break had only been a few days long. Even if he hadn't had a fiancée he was keeping under wraps, from her at least, what man would have flown all the way back from the other side of the world?

That was what she'd consoled her grieving heart with, anyway. Afterwards, after all the nights of weeping, when she'd recovered her equilibrium and had time to see it all in perspective. After the magazine article she'd stumbled upon in the doctor's waiting room about the wedding, when she realised what a fool she'd been, how much he'd deceived her. He probably agreed to trysts to meet women on towers all over the world.

Though at the time, on the *day*, she'd been green enough to believe that he'd keep the rendezvous. *She* certainly would have if she could. She'd been mad keen to go, clinging to the forlorn hope that he'd turn up like her own Cary Grant. If Fate hadn't intervened in that cruel way she'd probably still be there, texting the number that never answered, looking at her watch, wishing and hoping.

'Hey, darl, wake up.'

The voice of Josh, her colleague who occupied the desk opposite hers, snapped her back to the present. He leaned over and flicked her arm. 'What do you think he meant about us having to invest our free time?'

'There's no way *I'll* be doing that,' she said swiftly. 'What about Vivi?'

Josh tilted back in his chair. 'You won't have to worry. You'll be safe. Tell him you have a little mouth to feed and he'll take one look at your big blue eyes and crumble. Italians are crazy about kids.'

Something like a major earthquake redistributed her insides. 'Yeah?' she said faintly. 'Where'd you hear that? Surely every nationality is crazy about their kids.'

Josh's eyes, as blue as her own, were earnest. 'No, honestly. It's true. Genuine Italians—the real Italians from Italy—are particularly family oriented. I know, because there was an article about it in last month's *Alpha*.'

Amidst the laughter that followed, no one would have noticed that hers had a false ring. She'd read those things about Italians too. Their horror of broken families and children brought up without both parents. The sacrifices even the poorest of families were prepared to make to clothe and educate their children with the finest money could buy, as a matter of family honour. And what if they were a proud, aristocratic family? Would a *marchese* be happy to leave his child on the other side of the world?

Now that crunch time had arrived, *would* she be telling him about Vivi, and what exactly? The scenarios that opened before her if she did were frightening to contemplate. Six years were a long time. The things she'd understood about Alessandro then with such certainty were now all adrift. It was clear she'd never known him at all.

He had a right, of course, to know about his child. But what if he were one of those men who snatched their children and whisked them out of the country? Vivi wasn't a little tree who could be uprooted and transplanted across the world in London, or Venice. She was *five*, for heaven's sake. A *baby*. She only knew Newtown and her grandma, her school, the park… The King Street shops and the library, her little friends…

After Alessandro's reaction to her this morning, Lara needed to decide what to tell him, and how. Calm, brisk and unemotional would be best, of course, if she could *be* like that. The interviews could start at any minute. If she could just work out something she could say—maybe write it down and rehearse it…

Er… By the way, Alessandro, I think you should know… Incidentally, Alessandro, have I mentioned…?

The interviews started after morning tea. People either

came back with worried expressions, or exclaiming over things Donatuila had said. How sinister Alessandro was. How scary, how *gorgeous*.

They found themselves speaking in whispers. 'Oh, my God. Did you see his eyes? Those lashes are an inch long, I'll bet.'

'And his voice. That accent. What is it, London mixed with Italian?'

'That's not ordinary Italian. That's Sicilian. Betcha.'

A frightening rumour did the rounds that David from Finance had been told to empty his desk and given his marching orders.

The usual small congregation around the photocopier failed to materialise, and for once everyone resisted getting coffee from the machine between breaks to take back to their desks. Lara waited for her turn, struggling to work while she contemplated the things she would say to the stranger who was the father of her child.

She declined going out for lunch with the others. Her boots pinched her feet, and, anyway, who could eat?

Beryl's head jerked around Alessandro's door. 'Excuse me, Mr Vincenti, the builders are here.'

Alessandro thanked her, gave Tuila leave to break for lunch, then rose and stretched his long limbs before walking outside to meet the architect. He shook hands with the man, then they strolled along, discussing the layout of the rooms while the workmen wandered ahead, pencils tucked behind their ears, pointing out things about the wainscoting, measuring up floor space and window spans.

With the present layout, the rooms were too cramped, Alessandro explained, pausing outside the editorial office to indicate through the glass partition the number of desks crammed into the narrow space.

The room was empty of staff. Appeared to be, that was. Until, while the architect was examining the walls and suggesting ways of dealing with the problem, Alessandro caught sight of a blonde head bent over the coffee machine in the corner of the room.

That sensation again, as if something were crushing the air from his lungs.

He saw Lara Meadows turn to make some smiling response to one of the workmen, and for the second time that day the immediacy of her struck the chords of his memory like an assault. The pale fresh skin of her cheek. The grace of her hands…

That way she had of teasing a man with her laugh without any attempt to flirt. *Dio*, love the woman or hate her, her honesty and openness were still so appealing.

Despite the firewalls erected around his heart, desire, quick and hot, licked along his veins and stirred his loins with the old treacherous urgency.

To quell the bittersweet surge, he moved away from the partition. The architect talked and Alessandro listened, nodded, made the appropriate responses, all the while wrestling with devil fire. A temptation burned in him to take one more look at her, but he fought it. Steeling himself to ignore the craving, he concentrated on the conversation.

Discipline was what was needed. There was no denying her presence was a lighted fuse in his imagination. Now that he'd talked to her, seen her such a short distance from his office, he would have to think of a way to neutralise her effect. Regardless of his brain, his *will*, his body was plainly still in a time warp.

It didn't have to be difficult, he mused on the walk back to his office after he'd finished with the architect. The way was clear. Keep her at a distance until he was used to the idea of her again. Avoid hearing her voice, smelling her perfume…

Don't allow that laugh of hers to affect him. Don't give her the chance to beguile him with her wiles until he was ready for her.

Ready for her? an evil little unbidden voice chimed in. He was ready now.

Ridiculous, his reason stormed to defend the barricades. He was a civilised man. He'd never been a guy driven by his lusts.

Unless it was lust for Lara Meadows, the voice fired back with sly persistence.

Alessandro ran a finger around the inside of his collar. *Dio mio*, why had he come up with the interview scheme? Already she was invading his thoughts again, distracting him, infecting his bloodstream like a poisonous narcotic. The only way to ensure against her insidious way of creeping through the steel walls of his determination was to hold her at arm's length.

In fact, he should cancel her interview altogether. He had no desire to risk being alone with her again, had he?

As the afternoon wore on Lara's suspense grew. Everyone from Editorial had been invited except for her, and now people from other sections were being called in. Was Alessandro making her wait on purpose?

What if he expected her to stay after five to make up for her late arrival? Her mother would be waiting with Vivi, anxious to be released for her oboe lesson.

It was all very well for Signor Vincenti to insist on rules and punctuality. He wasn't a mother, with an eager five-year-old waiting for her dinner and bursting to share the excitements of her big day at school. Certainly he might, unknown to him by some quirk of fate, be a *father*, but in the current situation that was a mere technicality. In fact, from certain angles his ignorance of that small detail could be viewed as a plus.

For one thing it gave her a breathing space. Instead of her leaping to inform him at once, like a trusting fool, the responsible thing would be to suss out the lay of the land.

Weigh up his attitudes. See if he even *liked* children. After all, could she seriously contemplate inviting him into Vivi's life if he was likely to be a negative influence? And what about his wife? Vivi's stepmother?

She couldn't repress the cold sinking horror thoughts of the stepmother always invoked. What chance was there that a wealthy socialite would embrace her husband's love child with joy?

She'd had no way of keeping up with the state of their marriage. For all she knew, they might have other children now, children who would resent a surprise sister.

Perhaps Alessandro would feel the same way. After all, the world was thronging with men who had children from previous relationships and felt completely uninterested in them.

Out of sight, out of mind.

A situation like that could even be the most satisfactory solution for her and Vivi. Cause least disruption. No conflict, no expectations and no recriminations.

At thirteen minutes to five she gave up expecting to be called that day, and peeled off her boots to rest her aching feet for a few minutes before the walk to the bus-stop. It was eleven minutes to knock-off when a tall, dark form appeared in their doorway. All talk and action around her ground to a halt as everyone in the office froze to attention. Lara looked up and her eyes collided with Alessandro's.

From across the room a golden spark flared deep in his dark gaze and Lara felt an electric current frizzle the space between them and send a bolt of adrenaline zinging through her system.

'Lara,' Alessandro said. 'Can you come?'

For a second she sat paralysed by his brilliant, black-lashed gaze, then, like a being under the power of an irresistible force, she rose. Somehow disentangling herself from her chair and desk, she felt his glance slide down her legs to her feet.

Ridiculously, heat rushed to her cheeks as she realised she was still in her stockings.

'Oops,' she muttered, hastily grabbing for her boots. Sitting down to drag them on, she noticed Alessandro stare, then make an austere attempt to avert his eyes as if the sight were somehow indecent.

For some reason, she felt a surge of sheer exhilaration.

Let the married man flinch from the sight of her naked feet. It was the closest he'd ever get to any part of her ever again, naked or otherwise.

CHAPTER THREE

FOR the second time that day, Alessandro opened his door and gestured her in. Lara passed through, careful not to brush him, although all the fine hairs on her body stood up as if she'd passed by the open door of a furnace.

She felt relieved to see that Donatuila was absent.

The office wasn't very large, but for consultations with senior staff a space had been made over by the window for a cluster of armchairs.

After this morning's episode, she waited to be invited to sit, but Alessandro stood still for a moment, studying her with a veiled gaze, his mouth stern. Despite her taut resolve, when his eyes flickered from her mouth to her breasts her flesh responded with a willingness that was shamefully sexual, considering he was now off-limits.

This time she restrained her instinctive need to touch him, understanding at last that the old feeling of intimacy was a fraud. Gone now, just a ghost, though his once beloved face was still so familiar, confusing her emotions and whizzing excitement around her veins in the old chaotic way.

The silence lengthened, and with it her suspense. Forced somehow to break it, she started in proudly, 'Alessandro—'

He said quietly, 'You've grown your hair. Otherwise you haven't changed.'

Her hand made the involuntary flight to her nape. 'Yes. Yes, I have.'

He smiled for the first time, and it warmed his deep, dark eyes with the old devastating charm. 'You'll have to forgive me. I'm still a little jet-lagged. Of course, we have both changed. Please…' He indicated a chair.

She sat down, so relieved he seemed to remember her now, and was still the gentle, courteous man she knew. She resolved to respond in the same manner. Perhaps his coolness earlier had just been the result of surprise.

He took the chair opposite and opened a Manilla folder with her name on it. Her heart was thudding in a ridiculous rhythm, and to subdue the faint trembling of her hands she had to curl them in her lap. *His* lean, beautiful hands, though, were cool and steady, their supple strength reminiscent of the pleasure they'd once delivered. Such pleasures.

She dragged her eyes away. 'I couldn't believe it when they told us it would be you.'

'Couldn't you? Were you disappointed?'

'Disappointed? Well, of course not. I was just…just…'

'Nervous?' He gave an easy shrug. 'Don't worry. No need to defend yourself. This will be strictly business.'

The words struck a jarring note. She felt a rush of need to say something warm, to cut through the strangeness, but though he seemed relaxed, his movements smooth, something in his manner was controlled, as if a steel barrier resided beneath the polished surface.

She moistened her lips and glanced at her watch. 'I can't stay long. I have someone waiting.'

'Ah.' Though his voice was richly smooth, his eyes met hers with a penetration that cut through to her spinal cord. 'We mustn't let you keep anyone waiting.'

The corner of his mouth made a sardonic quirk, and she felt a stir of unease. Had there been a note of sarcasm there?

Alessandro lowered his gaze to her file, a tightening in his gut. Naturally, she would have someone waiting. Some un-suspecting clown. When hadn't she? He could hardly ask her who the lucky guy was this time.

He scanned the meagre notes, the arid lack of information. There was nothing of interest in her file, beyond a Newtown address and a phone number.

Her address was 37 Roseleigh Avenue. What could that tell a man? No clues as to what she'd been doing in the last six years. And with *whom*. Whoever had been in charge of Human Resources in this tinpot little company deserved to be sacked.

He stared at the page, willing himself not to look at her, though her image blazed through his eyelids. Her face had the same delicacy, that deceptively fragile beauty. There would be fools unable to help themselves from drowning in those deep-blue-sea eyes. Salivating for a taste of her ripe, deli-ciously resilient lips. She'd never be without a man. He should know how easy it was to be sucked into her fantasy world. To plunge into it.

Into her.

It was a risk, perhaps he felt as affected by her presence as he had earlier, but he allowed himself to skim a glance over her, feeling his blood-beat quicken despite his iron control. Whether he wanted it or not, that chemical connection was still dangerously potent, and he was as sure as he was of his name that she felt it too.

Though apparently relaxed, there was a tautness in her posture that suggested she was alert to the vibrations. Whenever she looked at him, her eyes were aware, the pupils just a little dilated, a sparkle in the irises. Surely they were bluer?

He forced himself back to the page. 'I see you started your job here in February.'

No doubt formality was the wisest approach, Lara thought, straining to interpret the signals. How could she have expected to fall into the same old easy-going way with him, after all that happened? Pity her body still didn't seem to get it.

'Yes, yes. That's right.'

She fielded the enquiries about her projects, increasingly conscious of the super-charged electric current connecting her to him at that visceral level. It had been too long for her. She must try not to stare, not to obsess on his gorgeous bones as if he were still hers, although she couldn't help noticing that his fingers were free of rings. Why? What had become of his wife? Or did he remove his wedding ring when he travelled?

She winced at the thought, then glanced at his face. Though his expression was shuttered, the grim line from cheekbone to shadow-roughened jaw discouraging, every instinct in her rose up against that possibility. Surely her perceptions of him six years ago couldn't have been so far off-target. Seeing him now in the flesh, so stern and hard and true, it was hard to believe he was anything but the decent and honourable man she'd believed in.

There had to be an explanation about the ring. Perhaps he and his wife hadn't exchanged them, though how likely was that? Giulia Morello was a socialite from a wealthy family, according to the magazine she'd read. It would surely be unusual for an Italian wife not to expect her husband to wear a ring.

As he questioned her about her work she examined him, drinking in the planes and hollows of his face, his cheekbones and strong black brows. She knew what it was like to kiss that mouth. Still so stirring to her starved imagination, the straight upper lip and slightly fuller lower lip were severely cut, and sensuous in a way that reminded her too well of times they had reduced her to quivering ecstasy.

She wondered if he felt the same hungry sense of possession she felt, as if her lips, her body should still belong to him, then felt ashamed of her wanton thoughts. Neither of them had a right to feel that way now.

Now that he had a wife.

'You have no former editorial positions listed. What other work have you done to qualify you for your present job?'

There was sensuality in the brilliant dark eyes devouring her face. At one time she'd have found that so invigorating. Maybe she still did, though—could she be imagining it, or was there an edge of underlying turbulence? But what was it? Violence? Anger? And whose anger? Hers, or his?

'Well, part-time work mainly, as an editorial assistant. Bill thought I had some rather good references from the publishing house where I started off. And I have done quite a lot of studies in literature. As you…as you might remember.'

She appealed to him with a smile, but he evaded it, lowering his gaze to hold her at a distance, as though any further mention of their former relationship was now forbidden. She supposed she should respect that, although he didn't have to be so cold.

Even—*hostile*.

She hastened to fill the silence. 'Bill seemed to think I was worth a chance with the children's book list. He…'

He looked up, irony in his intelligent dark eyes. 'He *liked* you.' That sexy mouth hardened. His gaze flickered to her throat.

'Well, yes.' She found herself sounding almost defiant, as if there had been an accusation wrapped in the words. 'I suppose he did.'

'Of course. He would.'

Though politely said, it didn't sound like a compliment. There was an uncomfortable pause, while she struggled to understand the implications. Was he suggesting that in some way she had cheated her way into Bill's good graces?

She felt as if the Alessandro she'd known was behind a barrier, as smooth and hard and slippery as glass. In an effort to reach him, she leaned forward a little, smiling and opening her hands in appeal. 'Look, Alessandro… It feels so strange, talking to you like this when we know—*knew* each other so well. How—how have you been?'

He raised his glittering black gaze to her. 'I think it would be best if you could forget our brief personal acquaintance. It's ancient history now. My task is to reform your company into a viable asset for Scala Enterprises. I prefer to focus on that.'

She recoiled as if from a slap. She bit her lip, and the blood came rushing up to her cheeks. 'Oh, right. Of course. Absolutely. If—that's what you want.'

Ancient history. Was that all she was to him? Why was he being so cold? Had he heard something about her? Or…was it something from the past? The remote possibility she'd occasionally entertained sprang into her mind, though surely not. He wouldn't have. Over and over she'd rationalised that likelihood out of contention.

He *wouldn't* have flown back because he'd never been serious about her. Five minutes after saying goodbye he'd married someone else.

She tried to read his face. 'Alessandro, is there something I'm not getting? I mean, I know it's a bit awkward us working temporarily in the same place, but it doesn't have to be a problem, does it? Surely we can…put aside…'

His black gaze flicked up to laser into hers for a long suspenseful second, then his mouth edged into an enigmatic smile. 'Our old liaison? Sure we can.' He made a lazy gesture with one lean, bronzed hand. 'Consider it never happened.' The dark eyes dwelling on her face were veiled, their lids heavy. 'As far as I am concerned, there was no summer idyll between lovers. *No* long afternoons of passion.' His glance drifted to her mouth. 'No lingering kisses, seducing our senses until we were drunk with each other. Forget that your lips ever touched mine.' He grimaced. 'Frankly, it's a relief to hear you take such a sensible attitude. Viewed in hindsight, these things often appear to have had a magic that is, in fact, deceiving. The most intelligent course for us now is to regard each other as strangers.'

'Strangers!' She flushed, warmed by the involuntary stirring of her body at his reference to those long afternoons, the kisses, at the same time hurt by the casual dismissal of the most passionate, the most heartfelt love she'd ever experienced with a man.

To be honest, the only love.

'I'm not sure I'll ever be that sophisticated. I don't think I can regard you as a stranger.' She added very sweetly, 'Though, of course, I'm not the one who got married.'

His thick black lashes swept down. There was a small, smouldering silence, as if a volcano brooded in some subterranean vault. As she waited for him to respond she observed his sexy mouth harden.

When he looked at her his black eyes were hard as jet.

'I think you are understating your ability to move on, Lara,' he said, his accent all at once very evident in his quiet, icy voice. 'However, much as I would love to dwell on the enchantments of undressing you in some long-ago hotel room, I have a mountain of work to get through.' As though unaware of her sharp intake of breath, he gave the file a little shake. 'So?' He lifted an aristocratic eyebrow to chivvy her along. 'Can we leave our personal issues aside? Shall we continue?'

His imperious tone set her hackles bristling. Was this the man she'd fallen in love with? She sat stiffly, her muscles clenched, and smouldered with resentment.

He cast her a veiled glance, then carried smoothly on.

'There's one thing that strikes me. I am curious. You have been with this company a short time, yet when last we met you were well on your way to an illustrious career in publishing. What have you been doing with your—*impressive* talents, apart from this part-time work as an assistant?'

That infinitesimal pause. The way he'd flicked down his eyelids on the word *impressive*. There had definitely been sarcasm there. She felt a surge of anger as an exquisite small face with big dark eyes, long luxuriant lashes and a halo of dusky curls rose before her.

Here it was. The moment of truth. The point to which all the tortuous pathways of her life had so far conspired to bring her.

Unfortunately, the moment hardly felt ripe.

She sat back and examined him. The Marquis of the Minor Venetian Isles was not the charming man she remembered. He was an icy, mocking, work-obsessed autocrat. Did he even deserve to hear what she could tell him, if she had a mind to?

She folded her arms under her breasts and smiled coldly. 'I don't want to bore you with the details of my little life, Alessandro. The truth is, I suspect that what I've been doing is probably too *personal* an issue to interest you. Suffice it to say I've done other things besides work in publishing.'

He narrowed his gaze to study her through his long lashes. 'There's no need to be defensive, Larissa.'

'Isn't there?' She wiped her smile, leaned forward and said in a low, trembling voice, 'You know, you aren't the man I remember.'

His brows shot up. 'No? Who do you remember?'

'Someone else. Someone—*kind*.'

His eyes glinted, but his expression remained hard and implacable, though she noticed a tiny vein jump in his temple. 'Whereas you, on the other hand, are exactly as I remember.' He added softly, 'To my regret.'

She gasped. 'Fine.' She gathered her bag, and, drawing her dignity around her, rose to her feet. 'In that case, I won't waste any more of your time.'

He sprang up as well, and to forestall him from opening the door for her and ruining her grand exit she turned quickly towards it. He must have lunged at the same time, for somehow his ankle hooked around hers, and their bodies entangled in an electrifying physical collision. It was like flint striking flint. At the points of contact at hip and thigh a high-voltage shock sped through her flesh, while the sudden blaze that flared in his dark eyes gave her a sensation of being showered in hot sparks.

Intensely aware of his arms whipping around to steady her, her deprived senses surged to the friction of his long, muscular thighs grazing hers, his evocative masculine scent and the strength of his big, iron-hard frame.

His hands slid to her upper arms, and he held her against him for a breathtaking moment that stretched into infinity.

'Careful, now.' His deep voice was a growl.

She was almost preternaturally conscious of the raw proximity of the hard body beneath the clothes brushing hers. Her mouth dried as her glance slid to his lips, and somehow those fire sparks in his eyes and voice must have crept under her skin, because she felt shaken all over.

Shaken and stirred.

Then abruptly, almost as if at some urgent signal, at the exact same instant they thrust each other away. She was left feeling giddy and disturbed, with a wild tingling in her breasts as though all her aroused blood cells were unwilling to lie down again.

'So sorry,' he said, a rasp in his voice. 'I don't know how that happened.' For a second his eyes were agleam as though he was about to say something more, but the nuance quickly vanished.

She pulled herself together and made for the door, then hesitated with her hand on the handle. His attitude about their past relationship had been so—negative, so repressive. But did she have to allow him the last word?

She turned proudly to face him.

He was back at his desk, tidying files and placing them in his briefcase.

'Alessandro?' That brush with him had given her voice an unwelcome huskiness.

He paused to glance up at her, one querying brow raised.

'There is something I need—to ask you. Something I need to get straight.'

'*Si?*' His eyes sharpened.

'Do you remember the pact?'

He stilled. For a full second it was as though his big frame had been snap frozen, and she had the scary sensation of having blundered onto a live mine. For a second his lean, handsome face might have been carved from ice.

Her heart began to tremble as his eyes narrowed on her face with a hard intensity.

'Pact?'

'The pact we made.'

His expression didn't change, but she was so sorry she'd mentioned it. How could she have offered it up for re-inspection in this hostile climate? But he was waiting now, and she felt condemned to plough on.

'You know,' she persevered in a breathless voice. 'When you had to go back to finish your studies at Harvard. The *deal*— that if we still felt the same way…' It was so embarrassing now, having to refer to their former feelings. 'If we thought there was a chance of us still—wanting to—be together, we'd meet in six weeks at the top of the Centrepoint Tower.'

He glanced down at the floor, a sardonic quirk to his mouth as if there were something nasty on the rug, then he looked up, his glittering eyes narrowed. 'Remind me. What was my part in this deal?'

'You—you agreed to fly back from Harvard in your mid-semester break.'

He considered her in silence, his eyes veiled, then his lashes drifted down. 'And *your* part was…?'

'Oh, well…' In truth, from a travel perspective she had always been shamefaced about the lightness of her end of the pact. From a certain angle, it could have looked to outsiders as though *her* sincerity was above reproach, whereas *his*…

Her lips dried with discomfort. 'I—I was to meet you there. Travel down from Bindinong.'

He strolled around to the front of the desk and leaned his big frame on the edge, his arms folded across his powerful chest, brows lifted.

'All the way from Bindinong?' he drawled softly, with a mockery that made her insides squirm. '*Sacramento*, I think it's clear who had the easier end of this deal.' There was a flash of something she couldn't interpret in the depths of those black eyes.

She wished she'd never brought it up. Certainly, Bindinong in the Blue Mountains wasn't that far from Sydney. When she'd lived there with her parents it had only been a ninety-minute train trip. Not quite as far as Harvard. Viewed now from the vantage point of maturity, the whole thing made the younger Lara Meadows look like some dewy-eyed tyrant, willing to put a man through hell to prove himself.

She made a small gesture of appeal. 'I know, I know it sounds unlikely from this distance, but at the time we both believed… We sincerely felt… Don't you remember?' As she tried to interpret his expression she felt herself growing hot. 'There were good reasons to make sure. You wanted me to go away with you—well, that's what you *said*—and I was young. I'd never travelled overseas, away from my parents. I was unsure, understandably, of risking everything for…'

'For me, apparently,' he said with a derisive lilt of his eyebrows.

It shook her, that he'd think of it, of her, in that hard way, then she started to see how the pact might have looked through his eyes, and felt all her doubts rise to the surface.

'And tell me…whose idea was it?' he continued the ruthless pressure. 'This—*pact*?'

He nearly spat the word. His uncharacteristic cynicism gave her a shock. Anyone would think she'd behaved badly. She had a flash of herself as acting like some capricious princess in a mediaeval fairy tale, setting endurance tests for her suitors.

So all right, he had been reluctant at first to agree, but he'd come to appreciate her reservations, and he *had* agreed. Heavens, who could expect a woman to just toss everything up and plunge into life with a man on just three weeks' acquaintance, without taking some time to think?

In the end, he'd seen the wisdom of her small delay, and

his acceptance of the pact had been as wholehearted and sincere as her own. Well, it had seemed so at the time. She had to keep reminding herself that it had all been a sham on his part. To look at him now, though, you would hardly think so, his expression was so hard and unforgiving.

'Well?' he queried.

'Oh, well...' What was this, the Spanish Inquisition? She could see by his stern mouth and the set of his handsome jaw that he wasn't about to admit to remembering it. 'Look, forget it. Just forget it. This clearly isn't the time.'

She made a move towards the door, but rocked to a halt when he said, 'So tell me, Lara Meadows. Did you? Keep your end of the deal?'

There was mockery in his voice and it caught her on the raw. She swung round to face him. His dark eyes were shimmering with a sardonic, enigmatic light.

'No. No, I didn't,' she said, anger welling in her at being mocked for what was, in fact, the tragedy of her life. 'And neither did you, or you'd have *known* that. You never had any intention of keeping it, did you?'

Ridiculous, after six years, but it still hurt. Just as well she was over him. Lucky for her she'd long since grown used to the idea that he'd never intended to come back. She'd just been a little diversion, to while away his time in Sydney.

All at once she had the most overwhelming need to leave. Run. Run as fast as she could from the gorgeous ice-man, all the way home, if necessary. Home to Vivi. Home to hug her darling little girl to herself.

All to herself.

But pride, and the need to keep talking, helped her keep her brave front. She gave a breezy wave of her hand. 'Just as well neither of us took it seriously. That was the deal, after all. No hard feelings on either side if anyone should pull out. Thank goodness we both did, or we'd really have something to regret, wouldn't we?'

She walked out on a cold, hard laugh, snapping the door to a little too firmly, and stood outside breathing more furiously than an Olympic hurdler, while the implications began to gel. How amused he'd be if he knew of the lengths she'd gone to in preparation for going away with him. If he had even the faintest idea how she'd loved him.

How she'd cried.

That was when she thought of the other thing she should have asked. Having gone so far to open the old wounds, she supposed she might as well know everything. How much worse could it get?

She opened the door again and looked back in. He was standing very still staring down at his files, his face a grim mask.

'Oh, incidentally, Alessandro,' she said softly, 'have you brought your *wife* with you?'

His head came up and he gazed at her for a long, steady moment, then a gleam shot into his eyes. 'My wife? I don't have a wife, *carissa*.'

It was her turn to stare. Then she realised what he'd said.

'Larissa,' she corrected, then with an exasperated gesture, 'I mean Lara. That's *Lara*.'

CHAPTER FOUR

LARA, Alessandro mused, standing under the shower in his hotel room, soaping his chest after a rigorous workout in the hotel gym.

For once he didn't feel like breaking into song. The interview hadn't been as satisfying as he'd expected. Using his power to punish a woman, however much she deserved it, hardly felt like the act of an honourable man.

He raised his arms and submitted himself to the jets of water, as if the warm needles coming from all directions could somehow rinse away the jagged feeling that had lodged somewhere just below his throat.

He forced himself to admit that, even with his perfectly justifiable anger, he hadn't relished hurting her. And strangely, despite the authority of his position as compared to hers, he couldn't honestly say he'd won the encounter outright.

That moment when she'd admitted her failure to meet him gnawed at him. He wasn't a fanciful guy by any means, but surely there'd been something in her manner then, that *look* in her eyes. Again, he canvassed the old possibilities he'd been through a million times, of her having been delayed on that fateful long ago day. As always, the inevitable question fired back. So why hadn't she phoned him to explain? Why had she made herself unreachable?

Even six years ago she could have messaged him, if she'd

been too cowardly to pick up the phone and eviscerate him voice to voice.

He turned off the shower and reached for a towel for a brisk drying off. There'd been that charge in the air when he'd met her today. *Dio*, it was so seductive, whether or not he wanted it to be. Towelling the springy black hairs on chest and long limbs with added vigour, he wondered if perhaps he should have confronted her with her treachery directly. Given her a chance to explain.

He dismissed the notion with an impatient growl. He might as well go down on his knees and show her what a fool she'd made of him.

Clean, dry and refreshed, he slipped on the thick hotel bathrobe and examined himself in the mirror, testing his beard. Was there any reason to shave? If he'd been seeing a woman this evening, he'd certainly have done so.

Perhaps that was what was needed. He should seek some feminine company and blot Lara Meadows out of his head.

The old solution. Not that it had ever worked.

He turned impatiently away from his reflection and strode into the sitting room and across to the mini-bar. There were miniature whisky bottles bearing quite a respectable label. He poured a shot into a glass and dropped in a couple of ice-cubes.

His corner suite had the advantage of large windows facing different directions, framing some quite breathtaking views of the harbour city. He stared broodingly out at the Opera House, radiating its startling beauty across the harbour, then strolled across to another window to survey the glittering light stream in George Street.

He supposed he could go out and taste the night culture, check out the wild-life, otherwise a long evening stretched ahead, empty of interest. Ironic that the only person he knew here, apart from Tuila, who'd arranged to stay with relatives, was the one least likely to want to spend time with him.

He sighed and swung away from the window. He'd chosen the Seasons because it was only a couple of blocks from the Stiletto building. Restaurants abounded in this old section of the city, so close to The Rocks and Circular Quay, but the thought of eating alone in some dim, intimate room designed for lovers didn't appeal.

He supposed he should order room service and start planning the staff allocations.

Another night, in another hotel.

Unless, of course, he phoned Lara now with some inquiry about the workings of Stiletto. He could suggest they meet, perhaps have dinner.

Per carità, where was his brain? He banished the idea in self-disgust. She'd know he was using a pretext, and when had Alessandro Vincenti ever needed a pretext to approach a woman?

And did he even want to risk sinking into that quicksand again?

Certainly, she was the only woman who'd ever rejected him, and in a particularly vicious, careless and cold-blooded way, but the physical fire *was* still there, regardless of what had happened six years ago. He felt his blood quicken at the memory of that amazing collision in the office.

If he'd kissed her then she'd have blazed like a torch. He'd have had her panting in his arms within seconds.

It struck him that if he had been affected by the encounter with her, she'd almost certainly be thinking about it too. He wondered what her current living arrangements were. There was the boyfriend she'd implied she had waiting for her, although could that claim have been inspired by pride? he wondered. A woman who lived with a man didn't make assignations to meet him after work. She simply went home to him.

An intriguing thought came to him. Perhaps she'd been so nervous of meeting him, she'd floated that excuse in case she'd needed an early getaway.

She might very well live alone.

He strolled back into the bathroom and placed his glass on the black marble vanity.

Now where was the shaving foam?

CHAPTER FIVE

COULD love be revived once it had been trampled on, betrayed and drenched in tears? Lara doubted it. While some elements of the old chemical reaction—the pounding heart, the weakened knees, the lust—could apparently still be stirred to action, they were echoes, doomed to fade in the harsh light of the present.

So why did she feel that the planet were suddenly spinning out of control?

The street lights were on by the time she opened her front gate. Newtown was the same rackety slice of bohemian life, the terrace house she and Vivi shared on different levels with her mother had the same slightly down-at-heel charm, but with Alessandro back in her life, however briefly, the world was suddenly vivid and exciting.

Although, she felt stung by that interview. Why on earth had she made it worse by bringing up the pact? Everything associated with it now was so painful. She'd only wanted to lay to rest that last minuscule worry that he might have flown all the way back from America and been disappointed, but her concern had only served to arouse his sarcasm. She'd had no idea—she was sure he'd never given any hint of resenting the pact so deeply.

Why should he have even given it two thoughts if he'd been planning to marry this other woman all along? Was that why he'd treated her so coldly today? He felt *guilty*?

She rested her bag of purchases from the Greek deli on the step, and pressed the doorbell.

Greta opened the door almost at once, accompanied by two cats and Vivi, who thrust herself forward for a hug, nearly knocking Lara backwards down the step with the fervour of her welcome.

'Nanna and me made pikelets, but I haven't spoiled my dinner and I haven't made myself sick yet,' she informed Lara earnestly, while Lara fought to set foot inside the foyer.

'I should hope not,' Lara said, laughing, hefting her up to hug her and give her a resounding kiss. 'And that's Nanna and *I*.' She turned to peck her mother's soft cheek. 'Sorry, I'm late, Mum. I was held up at work at the last minute. The—the new takeover team, and all that.'

'Good, good,' Greta said, her blue eyes lighting up. 'Any talent there?' then, seeing Lara's expression, 'Never mind, never mind. We live in hope. You can tell me all about it after dinner. I'm about to head off for my rehearsal.'

The groceries were retrieved from the step, Greta retreated to her apartment to put the finishing touches to her hair, and Lara and Vivi climbed the stairs to their floor.

Vivi really was amazingly like Alessandro, Lara thought, watching her daughter as she ran from room to room, reconnecting with all her precious possessions like a small, passionate whirlwind. She'd always known that, but now, after seeing him again in the flesh, the resemblance was striking.

Throughout the evening, every glance at Vivi confronted Lara with the seriousness of her dilemma.

After all the efforts she'd made to contact him during her pregnancy, she'd always imagined that if the moment of meeting him again eventuated, she'd be an honest, moral, upstanding woman and inform him of his responsibility straight away. She wasn't the sort to secrete her child, jealous of sharing, frightened of losing control. For goodness' sake, she'd never be one of those mothers who behaved like inflamed tigresses, dancing up and down on the side of the netball court, screaming advice to their daughters and hurling insults at the opposition.

She was calm and balanced. Protective and responsible, certainly. But mature. Rational.

Still, faced with the compelling reality, she found the issue was far more complicated than she'd expected. The truth needed to be faced. The Alessandro she'd met today was not the man she thought she knew. The father of her child was a stranger. One whose life was on the other side of the world.

There was no predicting how Vivi's life would change. How hers would. For goodness' sake, her baby was *five*. How could she cope with the shock of another parent?

Listening to her daughter's account of her day during the glorious ritual of the bath, Lara tried to work out how much to tell her mother. Of course Greta knew the *name* of Vivi's father, but Lara hadn't broken it to her yet about Alessandro's latest meteoric appearance in her life.

During dinner, watching Vivi carefully hide all her peas under a lettuce leaf then ease them off one by one to hide under her plate, Lara guessed what her mother's attitude would be. Tell him at once, Greta would urge. He deserves to know the truth. *Vivi* deserves it. And there was little doubt that he wouldn't be long at work before someone mentioned she had a child. As soon as he found out Vivi's age he wouldn't have to be a mathematical genius to work out the truth.

How dreadful for him if he found out in some casual conversation. If only he hadn't been so difficult this afternoon. So angry.

During the bedtime story, leaning back against the pillows with Vivi cuddled up to her and Kylie Minogie, her best doll, propped up beside them so she could see the pictures, every glance at her daughter over the pages of *The Little Mermaid* brought Alessandro's likeness forcibly before her.

The resemblance was in more than Vivi's dark velvet eyes and the richness of her hair. There was mischief and humour in that small face already, and even now the capacity for fathomless depths of…what?

Lara gave herself a little shake. Now she was being ridiculous. Vivi was only five. It was just the effect of having been with Alessandro after a long absence. Naturally his presence was overwhelming. Disquieting.

And admit it. In some way…energising.

It was a challenge. Not telling him would deprive Vivi unnecessarily of a parent, but on the other hand, the upheaval to their lives if he wanted to somehow participate in her parenting was frightening. How could he, anyway, from the other side of the world? It would be so unsettling and confusing, Vivi might be better off without him.

And today had been such a disappointment.

What had happened with the wife? she wondered, closing the story book and helping Vivi to settle down under the covers with Kylie Minogie. After his cavalier treatment of her she couldn't help wondering if he'd been a faithful husband.

There was no denying it. Whatever he was, whatever he'd *done*, the old fire had been breathlessly present in the vibrations between them. When he'd touched her in that accidental collision—and had it been accidental?—she'd felt stirred. All the way home on the train she hadn't been able to stop thinking of how disturbed that brief touch had made her feel.

Almost—aroused.

Her eyes drifted shut.

Though obviously, after six years of male deprivation, it was only to be expected he'd have had some impact.

She'd tucked Vivi into bed and had nearly finished the kitchen clean-up when the phone rang. Greta, she assumed, back from her oboe rehearsal and in need of a gossip.

She picked up the phone and cradled it between her ear and

her shoulder while she peeled off her rubber gloves. 'Hi, dear. Come straight up.'

There was a moment of silence, then, 'Do you say that to everyone who calls?'

She froze to the sink, her heart making a bound as his deep velvet voice trickled down her spine like liquid Tiramisu.

'Alessandro,' he prompted when she didn't reply at once.

Everything else in the world shrank and receded as the compelling tones thrilled through her. She managed to suck enough breath into her dislocated lungs to say, 'I know that.'

'We need to talk.'

She took the phone off her shoulder to hold squeezed in her shaking hand. Amazing, but even with her insides doing pirouettes, adrenaline cut in and she could speak.

'I can't imagine why,' she said coldly. 'But all right, then. Shoot.'

'Face to face.'

A shock of excitement raced through her. 'That's impossible. I'm not available tonight.'

'But you are at home.'

She glanced in the direction of Vivi's room. 'Well, yes, but I can't go out. I have—commitments.'

'Then I will come to you.'

She felt a bolt of alarm. 'No! You can't come here.' Anxiety helped her to unscramble her wits. 'Anyway, after today…the things you *said*…we can have nothing to say to each other. We're strangers, remember?'

He said swiftly, 'But you don't accept that. I'm certain that was what *you* said.' And when she didn't answer added, 'You know there are things we need to discuss.'

That was rich, after the way he'd refused to acknowledge their former relationship.

'Things. Oh, you mean things about *work*?'

'What else?'

Her heart was thundering. Yeah, right. Things about work indeed. If he wanted to know operational things, he could ask anyone. And he could wait until tomorrow. Did he think she was an idiot? He wanted to *see* her.

Oh, God. Forget all the negative emotion and confusion of the day. Face the truth. That mesmeric connection was still there. The excitement. And she wanted to meet him. God, she wanted to. If she could arrange to meet him somewhere…

He said firmly, 'I'll be in your street in a couple of minutes.'

'What?' she gasped, but it was too late. She'd spoken into dead space.

Immediately, she phoned down to Greta's, but her mother mustn't have returned yet. Then she realised she was wearing track pants and a ragged old sweater that had borne the brunt of too many bathtime splashes.

She dashed to her bedroom and dragged on her good jeans and a top. Though surely the red top was too clingy? What sort of a statement was it making? One breath of cold air and her nipples would stand up and protrude through the layers. Quickly she whipped it off and dived into her wardrobe for a shirt. She shrugged a sleeveless vest over it, ran a brush through her hair and smoothed on some lipstick.

She ran to the front window, and gasped when she saw a dark car pulling up across the street from the house. She jumped back, and stood for seconds, dithering. She'd open the door to him, and talk to him on the porch. In a worst-case scenario, she could invite him into Greta's as if it were *her* place.

Unless…

She thought rapidly. Unless Vivi had left toys there. And there were the photos.

If he came *here*, her bumpy heartbeat told her, if he saw Vivi, she'd have no time to prepare. No time to prepare Vivi, no time to break the news gently to him. Somehow, she would have to lure him away from the house.

Her hands twisting, she paced back and forwards, stopping

several times at Vivi's door to glance in, dashing in once to ensure the covers were in place over the slight mound of her daughter's sleeping form.

The downstairs bell to Greta's flat gave a couple of sharp peals, and, torn between rushing to answer it and defending her cub, like a maddened tigress Lara dashed in to resettle the covers over Vivi's shoulders.

CHAPTER SIX

ALESSANDRO surveyed No. 37 with curiosity. Third in a long row of Victorian terraces, its street frontage was narrow, and like the others it appeared to have two levels, with balconies at both. A creeper trailed from the ornate iron lace of the upper balustrade. The street was pleasant, the plane trees along its pavements bare, their last leaves now adrift after having succumbed to the southern wintry air.

Light glowed in an upper-floor window, and he thought he could see a figure flit past the filmy curtain. Lara, he thought, the buzz quickening in his blood. As he was about to leave the rental car a cruising taxi slowed and drew up in front of the house, and he stilled, his hand on the door handle.

A woman alighted. She was wearing a bulky coat, and in the glow of the street lamp gave the impression of being of mature age. She was carrying some sort of case, perhaps a musical instrument. She bent to speak to the driver, then walked into Number 37 and up to the front door, where she took a moment to search her handbag, then let herself in. A light came on in a ground-floor window.

Alessandro gave her a moment, then got out and crossed the street.

He didn't have long to wait after ringing the bell before the woman answered. She wore her wheat coloured hair swept into a bun, and though her warm, attractive face was more lived in than Lara's, he detected an unmistakable resemblance in the fine bones and resolute chin. Shrewd, humorous sky-blue eyes looked him up and down and measured him all the way through to his soul.

Ah. The mother.

Still, he realised with a surge of triumph, no boyfriend on the premises. There almost certainly would not be a boyfriend.

'Alessandro Vincenti,' he informed her, with a courteous inclination of his head. 'Is this where Lara Meadows lives?'

For a second the woman stood stock-still, then her eyes shone with an intense silvery light. 'Ah. Yes. Yes, it is indeed. If you wait here I'll just get her.' She turned back inside, then gave a small start and exclaimed, 'Oh, here she is now. Lara, someone to see you. Ales—Excuse me, now—did you say your name was *Alessandro Vincenti*?'

Alessandro assented with a grave murmur.

From the top of the stairs Lara heard Alessandro's voice in conversation with her mother's and she felt her stomach lose its floor as all her separate universes collided.

Somehow she managed the walk down without tumbling.

Alessandro was even more darkly gorgeous on her door-step. He looked taller, more sophisticated, more thrillingly, exotically Italian. As she paused halfway down he lifted his dark gaze to hers and she felt the old adrenaline kick higher.

Her watery knees held. *Just.*

He'd changed into a casual jacket and trousers with a black polo sweater. The black—surely it was cashmere—enhanced his olive colouring and deepened his eyes to shimmering brilliance. As they swept over her in masculine appraisal the sensual golden flicker in their depths touched a trigger somewhere deep in her abdomen.

'Hi.' If only she could sound normal, *not* be so conscious of her breasts, despite their heavy-duty shield, she could deal with him. Fear of blushing prevented her from looking at her mother, but she still felt the heat rise through her neck and ears.

She said breathless, useless, stilted things.

'Well, er—Alessandro, how are you?'

'Fine. And yourself?'

'Fine, fine. Did you…did you have any trouble finding the house?'

'None whatsoever. I have the—what do you call it here?—GPS.'

She saw him glance at her mother, and said quickly, 'This is my mother,' then turned to Greta to explain—as if it *could* be explained that the big boss of the company had headed straight to her house on his first night in Sydney—'Alessandro has come to—to manage Stiletto. He—he wants to ask some questions about the company.'

She blushed outright then at the unlikeliness of it, and with mixed emotions saw Alessandro take her mother's hand and say in his beautiful accent, 'It is charming to meet you, Signora Meadows.'

Though her mother's response was restrained, Lara could tell she was ravished to her kneecaps. And absolutely undeceived.

Lara threw him a sardonic glance, knowing he was fully aware of the effects of his high-voltage courtesy on Australian women, and his dark gaze met hers with bland inscrutability. Before her mother could start inviting him to dinner and making offers of accommodation, Lara cut in, 'Oh, goodness, Mum, I've just thought. Would you mind going upstairs to—to make sure I turned the iron off?'

Greta looked startled, but Lara tweaked her sleeve and added, 'Just to make sure everything's all right up there, please, dear. If you wouldn't mind?'

Greta's eyes lit with comprehension. 'Certainly dear. Of course. We don't want to set fire to anything. Bring Alessandro inside out of this chilly air.'

Lara waited until her mother was out of earshot, then said in a low voice, 'Well, I did tell you not to come, but since you're here now, what is it?'

His glance assessed her and pierced straight through her defences. Her vest might as well have been made from gauze. 'Relax, *bambina*. Let's not keep up this pretence we aren't pleased to see each other. Have you had dinner?'

She folded her arms in front of her. 'You're kidding yourself there. Why would I want to see someone who's a cold, arrogant—?' She broke off, unwilling to frame the word.

He smiled, and it lit his eyes, his whole face, with warmth. 'Bastard is the word you're looking for. For the same reason I might want to see someone who's a defensive little liar.'

Her insides lurched in shock. What did he mean? Had he heard something about Vivi already? Then she saw that his eyes were still smiling and her heart dropped back into its niche. 'Anyway,' she said quickly to ease over her scare, 'we've already—we've had dinner.'

He looked surprised. 'So early?' He paused a second, as if perhaps waiting for Greta's invitation to be reissued. She felt slightly ashamed to have to be so inhospitable, when *his* manners were usually so excellent. When she said nothing he tilted his head towards the end of the street. 'I noticed a brasserie somewhere along there. Come, then, we'll have a glass of wine.'

Truly, after the way he'd treated her at work, he had a nerve. It had clearly never occurred to him that she might refuse. And to be honest, it didn't seriously occur to her. Despite all her fears and anxieties, it was abundantly clear that the moment of revelation had arrived and there was no avoiding it.

At least he'd decided to abandon hostilities. For the conversation she had churning around in her mind the atmosphere needed to be calm. Pleasant. Rational.

As she would be, once her heart had slowed down a little. Once the wild old excitement in her veins had stopped its seething. Was it so weak of her to relish the rare heady pleasure of being seen in public with a stunningly attractive man? She felt sure any woman who'd pushed a pram single-handedly would appreciate the allure of it.

Praying fervently that the man-rich air hosties who lived across the street were watching through their front windows, she unhooked her jacket from the stand inside the door and slipped it on.

He was standing outside the gate, gazing interestedly around at the neighbourhood.

She closed the gate behind her and he cast her a dark, inviting glance that thrilled through her like ocean spray. She walked along the street with him, under the bare trees and the old street lamps, past the rows of terraces with the minuscule front gardens inside their iron railings, trying not to show how she savoured every rare, precious step.

How she'd dreamed of this. How many times had she pushed the stroller to the shops and fantasised that her lover would come back for her and his little girl?

He adjusted his long strides to hers on the uneven pavement, just as he had the last time he'd been in Sydney. He was a true Venetian, he'd explained to her then. Walking around cities was one of his favourite pastimes. This was how it had all started, those magic walks.

That time came back to her then with such a powerful intensity, she felt quite tremulous and emotional. Occasionally the back of his hand, his shoulder, his hip made an accidental contact with hers, and the joyous old electricity shivered through her. She made herself widen the distance between them, glanced up at the cold night sky as if the distant Milky Way could distract her, not that it was visible in the glare of the city lights, but her desperate flesh yearned for more of those delicious little brushes.

She'd lived like a nun for too long, that was the trouble. It had weakened her defences against tall, handsome Italians with smiling eyes. But she needed to keep her head. Whatever she said tonight would be inscribed in stone for keeps.

His dark gaze captured hers. 'I am surprised to see you're still living with your parents. I thought—isn't Bindinong in the Blue Mountains?'

She nodded. 'After Dad died Mum and I moved to Sydney.'

He stopped in the middle of the pavement. 'You've lost your father. I'm so sorry to hear that. Was this an illness? Or…?'

'No, no. He—he died in a bushfire. It was that really hot summer.' She glanced quickly away from him, the words drying on her tongue. She couldn't tell him so bluntly, not like this, and open it all up again. She drew in a breath, and finished curtly. 'Their house burned down. We lost—just about everything. Afterwards, Mum wanted to start life afresh in another place.'

'*Per carità.*' He looked genuinely shocked, and stood shaking his head in dismay. 'But that's a terrible tragedy.' Gazing at her with concern, he touched her cheek with his knuckle.

It was only a light touch, but tender. As always when the disaster was mentioned and someone showed sympathy her throat thickened. She lowered her swimming gaze and quickly turned away. Tempted again to spill all of it at once, make a dent in his smooth armour, she drew breath to speak. Then she remembered his coldness earlier, his mockery, and thought better of it. Enough that it had happened *when* it had happened.

There was no point telling the man who'd married someone else how the family tragedy had interfered with her plans to *be* with him. Why whip him with it just to leave herself exposed?

And she had something more precious to lose than mere pride.

As if in mockery of her inner struggle, he took her arms in his strong, gentle grip. 'I am so sorry about your father, Larissa.'

Her senses plunged into uproar. Oh, the temptation to melt against him and soak up the comfort of his arms. With his use of the affectionate name he used to call her, his dark eyes glowing with such genuine concern, he was almost the sincere, charming man she'd fallen in love with.

He could do that so well, her brain reminded itself, make a woman believe he cared, *such* beautiful manners, while on another level some primitive part of her was alive to something else in those dark eyes. Some hot, fiery spark in their depths that had nothing to do with the conversation.

Her heart skipped up a gear. A kiss was in the offing. More than a kiss. If she once glanced at his mouth, it would happen, the moment would intensify, and then...

'It *was* a—a tragedy,' she acknowledged, stiff in her effort not to let her eyes stray. 'But Mum and I got through it. We had each other. We had—good things to live for,' she added hoarsely, disengaging herself in time.

Was he aware of the galloping vibrations, her voice, the sudden tension? He walked silently for a few metres, then gave her a long, subtle glance, brimming with sensuality, his gorgeous sexy mouth not quite edging up at the corners, and her insides did a slow flip.

He knew. Of course he knew.

They turned the street corner into the main shopping precinct. As always any time of the day or night, Newtown was humming with its own offbeat energy. Patrons thronged the bars and theatres, spilled onto the pavement from the multicultural mix of cafés, protected from the chill night air by clear plastic walls, while late shoppers still lingered at the delis and the organic green co-op. In the doorway of the Friends' Design Gallery, a dreadlocked man with a sax sat before a brazier playing 'Unchained Melody', in competition with the sound of bouzoukis issuing from the Greek restaurant further along the street.

She shoved her hands in her pockets and hugged the coat to herself. She wasn't so aware of being cold. Nerves and the excitement of being out in the night air were making her tremble on the inside of her skin. Or perhaps it was what she had to tell him.

She hoped he was in a mood for revelations.

The brasserie had awnings on the windows and a softly lit bar at one end, with tall bar stools and a couple of tables in inviting little alcoves with plush banquette seats. Logs blazed in a giant fireplace set into the middle of the floor, screening most of the bar area from the main restaurant. It was inviting, and in one of the alcoves a group lingered over their pre-dinner drinks, soaking up the warmth.

Alessandro steered her to the other table. She slipped off her coat and sat down, and he slid into the seat at right angles to hers. He picked up the wine list, and with a glance at her edged a little closer so she could examine it with him. She scanned the list, aware of feeling the heat from his body, intensely conscious of their arms touching, his ribs just a few inches away from hers.

The bartender was doubling as waiter in the restaurant, so they had plenty of time for consultation. Not that she knew anything about wine, and throughout the discussion she sensed another kind of communication between her and Alessandro that kept her heart drumming. Made her careful to avoid too much eye contact.

Eventually the waiter materialised and Alessandro ordered a merlot, then lounged back against the banquette, his eyes making occasional flickering glances to her face and hands, lingering on her throat. She'd rarely felt more conscious of her body. Was it like this for everyone who met an ex-lover? Once having been activated, were those old triggers for ever present and at risk of causing their owners to burst into flame?

When the rich crimson wine was before them, he clinked glasses with hers.

'*Salute.*'

She met his eyes, and they were veiled, with golden shimmers of heat in their dark depths that she recognised with a deep pang of response. His movements were measured, his mouth relaxed, and so stirringly sensual and evocative of past pleasures, she had to lower her gaze.

This was how he'd looked before, when love was on the menu. When he'd been confident of her. He was at his most devastating, but it was important she keep command of herself. Not allow herself to be seduced.

She thought of Vivi. How warm would he be when she told him?

He watched her take a sip, the firelight reflected in his eyes, then he angled his body a little further her way. 'So fill me in on your little life. Is there a guy?'

The question sounded lazy, but despite his sleepy eyelids and relaxed tone there was a stillness in him as he awaited her response. It was tempting to lie, tease him a little. Pretend she was as desirable to other men as she'd once been to him. But how sad would that be? It had been her choice to lead the celibate life. The search for a partner was too hard. A series of uncles while she reviewed their qualifications was not what she'd planned for her daughter.

'Not currently.'

His black brows lifted. 'Why not?'

She swirled the wine in her glass, then sipped, welcoming its rich mellowness on her dry lips, aware of his glance drifting to her mouth. 'Is there ever an answer to that question?' She lowered her lashes, then looked up again, directly at him. 'What about you? Is there a woman?'

He shook his head. 'No woman in particular.'

'But—you *had* a woman,' she said silkily. 'Your wife.'

He frowned down at the table. 'For a very short time. That was—a mistake. We married each other for—reasons we shouldn't have.' He looked grim all of a sudden, and she felt a little flare of anger. The thought came to her, not for the first time, that he should never have married that woman. He'd belonged to *her*.

'You must have already known her when you were here before,' she said lightly. 'With me.'

He gave a shrug. 'Since childhood.'

She felt a sort of helplessness, imagining their intimacy, the shared experiences of long acquaintance. How could she ever have competed with that?

'Did you tell her about—me?'

He met her gaze steadily. 'Everything.'

'And she still went ahead with the wedding?'

His eyelids flicked down, and she thought suddenly she would never understand. Never be able to guess how aristocratic Venetians and their wealthy connections thought about such things as love and marriage, and little flings on the side.

It cost her some pride, but she had to ask. 'Did you love her?'

He scanned her face, his dark eyes glinting. 'Whatever I say to that you will hold against me, one way or another.'

'Then you did.' She smiled, though it scraped her heart.

'I'm beginning to feel flattered. What do you care?'

'I don't care,' she said fiercely, her voice shaking all at once. She set down her glass with a snap.

Unexpectedly, he leaned over, tilted up her face and took her lips in a hot, hungry little kiss. The contact with his sensuous mouth was electrifying. While her mind reeled in shock, her parched lips responded to the delicious friction like the desert earth drinking in the rain. As he intensified the connection, gripping her with one lean hand on her ribs, fiery tingles set her mouth alight, and a hot, sweet, overwhelming rush of desire whooshed straight to her nipples.

She should have resisted, but he slipped his tongue inside her mouth with the clever old artistry, tangling it with hers and igniting the tender tissues inside. As his hot breath mingled with hers she could have swooned with all the fantastic sensations, not least being the inflammatory effects on her erotic imagination.

While the masculine taste and scent of him flooded her starved senses, her breasts warmed and strained against the fabric of her bra, all her erogenous zones bursting into vibrant, throbbing life.

Just when she was ready to climb on his lap, wrap herself around him and make the leap to the next steamy level, a background noise impinged on her ears, and, as if suddenly mindful of the place, Alessandro released her and they jolted apart.

Barely awake to the real world, she glanced about, but to her relief no one was in direct view, other drinkers having long vacated the bar, and the bartender/waiter busy in the restaurant. Hot, flushed and aroused, she turned a reproving glance on Alessandro, and felt scorched by the desire in his wolfish gaze.

Oh, God. Her racing heart started to thunder a warning. It was happening again. The most dangerously seductive man on the planet, and here he was, sweeping her along again, hypnotising her until her brain cells spun into cotton candy and her responsibilities all floated out the window.

Overloading her senses. Fogging her brain.

Wasn't this the same pattern, unfolding just as it had before?

A conversation. A pleasant *walk*. Those first light touches—the casual brushing of shoulders, hand to cheek, hand to hand. A soft stroke of her hair.

That first tender kiss.

Then the deeper kisses. The hotter, more passionate kisses. The wild, hungry, desperate kisses with the insane, thirsty cravings for skin contact…

The hotel room… Oh, God, the hotel room.

And then the obsession.

And this time, *this* time, he'd omitted some steps to jump straight in at hot and sexy. Except this time she had more than just herself to think about and she really did need to resist.

So how? With all she had to lose, how *could* she have allowed herself to succumb to his first move so easily?

She needed to be strong. Cool, tough and in control. Show him she wasn't affected by his ploy, masterful though it had been.

She marvelled at the breathtaking ease with which he'd managed to transform the mood of the strained afternoon meeting from hostility to lust. And she'd plunged right in.

In an attempt to minimise her compliance, she fought to calm her breathing and gain control of her voice. With her blood still pulsing through her like a rapid river, she forced some brain cells to reassemble, and managed a croaky, 'Look,

Alessandro, what are you doing? Do you think you can just take up where you left off? I have a different life now, I'm a different person. You're only here for a few days, and there is something I need to—'

His eyes darkened. He took her hands and it was like connecting to the power grid.

'You taste the same.'

The warm, smooth grasp, the piercing, sensual gleam in his eyes played on her desire and weakened her resolve, but it was too confusing, arousing, and there was her pride. Only minutes before he'd been talking about his wife. And she couldn't afford to take any more risks with her heart, not with Vivi to consider.

Vivi. She snatched her hands back.

'Forget about my—*taste*.' She nearly gasped the word. 'There's something important I need to tell you.' She glanced at her watch. 'And I can't be late home. Mum's working tonight.'

'Work? At this hour?'

'She's a midwife. This week her shifts start at eleven. She likes to—' She waved her hand impatiently. 'Forget about that.'

Encountering sensual amusement in his dark eyes, she had the nervous realisation that she was about to deliver him a jolt that would wipe away his insouciance. He politely elevated his brows.

Despite her anxiety a false calm came over her, courtesy of a massive surge of adrenaline. She could do this. She had to, for Vivi's sake.

Straightening her spine, she said in a steady voice, 'As it happens, I have a child.'

Her quiet words seared the air like nuclear fission.

Alessandro grew very still, though something stirred in the dark depths of his eyes. The silence stretched. 'Is that so? A child?' He lowered his lashes, and when he glanced up again, his gaze had sharpened to a cool, wary probe. 'I'm surprised you didn't mention it sooner.'

All her muscles were tense. 'I know. I would have, but, as I said, I found it impossible to contact you.'

Somehow his lean, powerful frame grew even more still, as though carved in ice. Then he blinked, echoing, 'To contact me.'

She gazed wordlessly at him, her pulse drumming in her ears, and saw comprehension flood his eyes.

He closed them in disbelief. '*Sacramento.*' He held up a hand as if to hold her at bay. 'How—*old* is this child?'

'Five.'

'What are you saying? Are you trying to tell me it is—*my* child?' The long, idle fingers on his glass tightened convulsively.

She met his gaze squarely. 'Yes, Alessandro. She is.'

Alessandro felt a numb sensation in his chest. He searched her blue eyes for signs of faltering from her assertion, but they were steady and unwavering. A darker, more shadowy blue, perhaps. Troubled, even. But honest, true and definite.

'But—' He felt an urgent need to hold the news at a distance before he examined it closely. 'You would have told me this.' He gripped her arm. 'Surely, you would have told me.'

'I would have, if I could.' One delicate eyebrow raised, she glanced down at his encircling fingers, and he released her arm at once. Shock. It must have been the shock. Almost unconsciously she rubbed the spot, then shrugged and spread her hands. 'As I explained, you weren't at Harvard when I called.'

'No, I know, but—you knew I worked for Scala Enterprises. You could have phoned the head office. Sent a letter.'

'I did send a letter to the office in Milan, where you'd worked before. *Said* you worked. To be honest, I wasn't sure if any of the things you'd said were true.' He flushed with anger, and she added, 'You must realise, when I read about your wedding…'

His eyes flashed. 'Ah, now I understand. *That's* why you didn't contact me. Because of Giulia.'

She felt her own anger rise. 'Well, what do you expect? Would your bride have welcomed the news? Would *you*?'

'Possibly not, not at that stage.' His lean, handsome face had hardened to a stern, proud mask. 'But you didn't have the right to make that judgement. It was not up to you to decide what *I* should do in regards to a—a *child*.'

Her heart was thumping, her blood furiously eddying along her arteries like Rocky River rapids. 'All right, then, what would you have done if you'd found out? Would you have wanted her in your life?'

He gazed at her, his eyes brimming with some fierce, dark emotion, and bit out, 'You have no idea, do you? No idea.'

'I don't, no.' She took a swallow of wine in hopes of calming her shaking voice. Not to reveal her excruciating fear. But driven by what she knew she must say, even if it meant offering up her darling, she said hoarsely, 'So what now, then? Now that you know. Do you intend to participate in the parenting? Be her father?'

He looked stunned, as if such an idea had not even occurred to him. 'Participate?' He shook his head, growling, 'How can I? My base is in Europe. I travel. *Constantly.* I do not…I am not the sort of man who…' His eyes were glittering, his lean hands so expressive of his inner disturbance. 'This needs to be considered. Of course you will need money. That is easy—no problem, but as for this—this *parenting*… What are you expecting? What do you want from me?'

'Nothing.'

The blunt word erupted from the recess of fear in her heart with a sincerity that didn't escape Alessandro, judging by the swift upshoot of his brows and a look in his eyes that suggested he was more than merely taken aback.

He looked as if he'd sustained another shock.

'Sorry.' She spoke rapidly, regretting her unfortunate outburst. 'That sounded a bit blunt. I just want you to understand that it doesn't have to be the end of your life as you know it.' She evaded his eyes. 'I'm not asking for anything from you. It's probably not the same here as it is where you come from.

People aren't expected to make unwelcome marriages, so you can relax. You don't have to rush me to the altar.' He drew breath as if to speak, but she held up her hand to forestall him. 'Just in case you're wondering, you've got no chance.' She summoned up the ghost of a smile. 'It's too late now, anyway. My reputation is already ruined.' She stared down at her twisting hands. 'We—like the way we are. Mum, me and Vivi.'

His stunned look receded. He sat in smouldering silence, a glint in his narrowed gaze, his mouth a grim sardonic line.

All at once he swallowed the last of his wine and rose to his feet. 'Let's get out of here.'

CHAPTER SEVEN

OUTSIDE, striding along the pavement with Lara at a pace in tune with his musings, Alessandro drew deeply of the night air, as if the chill might calm his desire to smash something. There were issues to be considered here, and he wasn't likely to fight his way through if his blood was fired with unnecessary emotion.

He needed a cool, sharp brain. Illogically, Lara's revealing response to his query had jabbed at him. He knew very well 'nothing' hadn't meant nothing from him. It had meant nothing *of* him. He gritted his teeth. He shouldn't allow himself to be bothered by that. He was over all that negative fallout from the past. So she'd made it clear she didn't want him in her life—*their lives*—why did that have to make him feel so raw?

Obviously, from a rational viewpoint, no contact at all would be better for the child than meaningless attempts at an insincere relationship that could never develop. If her mother was happy to raise the infant without making any demands of him, it was surely a matter to celebrate.

And maybe the child *would* be better off. What would he have to offer a child?

He glanced at Lara's slender jean-clad form hurrying along beside him and once again the wave of unreality engulfed him. Unbelievably, she'd been pregnant, made pregnant by *him*. He tried to imagine her swollen with his child, and felt a bizarre quickening of his pulse. For a crazy instant he wished he could have seen that, smoothed his hand over her round belly, felt the full, milk-laden breasts. He shook off the sensuous image. *Dio*, was he sick?

Only a few minutes ago he'd been lusting after her as though no time had ever elapsed, contemplating whizzing her back to the hotel and taking the erotic curves and hollows of her gorgeous body back into his glorious animal possession.

He felt his abdominal muscles clench in a silent groan of loss. Desire had to be the last thing on his mind now. She was a mother, while *he* was…

Sacramento. A father.

The irony of it. What sort of a father could he ever make, with his experience?

Scenes from the nightmare segment of his own childhood lurked in the corners of his mind, threatening to storm centre stage, until with a bracing of his will he banished them back to the hell where they belonged.

One thing he could be sure of. Whatever the rights and wrongs of it, the moral issues, the woman's needs, he knew with all his heart that Fate had decreed some men should never be entrusted with the care and nurturing of little children. It was well documented that people behaved as parents as they themselves had been raised.

Though… Some opposing instinct sprang forward to conflict with the sickening suggestion. Surely it could not always be the case. Who was to say he would follow the pattern of his stepfather, when it had been his life's work to be the antithesis of that weak, violent man?

Would he ever be driven to vent his nightly rage and fury on a woman or a child? A little girl? He couldn't imagine himself. He'd felt plenty of anger on occasion, even fury a couple of times, but he'd never experienced a need to damage and punish others.

Almost certainly, his instinct grasped at the assurance his mother had given him. He'd always held fast to her assertion that he took after his real father, that tall, gentle figure who was no more than a shadow on the edge of his memory.

But what if he were wrong? What if he'd absorbed the poison into his child's soul?

'Alessandro.' He became aware of a tug at his sleeve. 'Slow down a bit. Do you mind? I'm having to run to keep up.' She smiled, though there was a ruefulness in her blue eyes, as if she guessed at his turmoil.

Impossible. She'd made it clear she hardly knew the slightest thing about him. If she had, if she knew how much he'd wanted her, *yearned* for her, would she have dismissed him so carelessly that long-ago summer?

He made a wry mental grimace. And here she was, doing it again.

Still, he slowed his steps and presented his cool, smooth face. 'Sorry. I was forgetting. I'm… There's—a lot to think of.'

'I know. Look… Look, I'm sorry to have been so tactless in the telling of it. I know this must have come as a terrible shock.'

'It is a shock, certainly.' But terrible? Did it have to be? That maverick thought jumped out at him, glimmering, mysterious, and he shoved it to the back of his brain to dwell on later.

As though sensing the explosive nature of his silence, she continued a nervous stream of chatter, her words misting on the night air. 'You'll want to have the DNA testing done. I'm ready for that, of course, though you'd never have any doubt if you saw…'

He stopped still and held up his hand. 'Please. If I'm to have minimal contact with this—situation, it's better you don't tell me any details about it.'

He felt himself flush, knowing he had sounded cold, inhuman even. He could sense her shock, but it was better for all their sakes if he didn't have to think of the child as a person. Her eyes widened at his clipped tone, but then she nodded in hasty agreement.

A chill like ice settled in his chest. How ironic, that the woman he'd desired above all others was anxious only to see the last of him. 'I'll—investigate the testing procedure here and do my part separately,' he said, a little less curtly. 'I believe we can—co-ordinate the process.'

'All right. Fine.' She glanced at him in appeal. 'Please, Sandro, don't be so angry. You look like a thundercloud.'

Her use of his affectionate name stung like crazy, and brought all his resentment and outrage back to the surface. He expelled an incredulous breath and turned to her, flinging out his hands. 'What do you expect, Lara? You have kept a child—My... *My*—' He smote the air. '*Hidden* for five years. I am—' He reefed a hand through his hair. 'I am blown away. Of course it's a shock. It's a *responsibility*.'

'Well, I think I know something about that.' There was an emotional tremor in her voice.

He stopped and grabbed her arms, forcing her to face him. He could feel the life force pulsing through her slim, vibrant flesh. 'This wasn't how it had to have been, though, was it, *tesoro*? You could have had my support. If you'd wanted to... If you'd really tried you could have contacted me.'

'I did really try. Do you think I *wanted* to be alone?' Her mouth twisted and there was a vulnerable quiver in her voice. She lifted her hands and gave him a little push.

He turned away, unwilling to imagine the difficulties she must have endured, the hardships. Unwilling to acknowledge... Oh, *Dio*. He was flooded with the most excruciating guilt.

For an instant he covered his eyes with his hand, swamped by the damning images. Her beauty on that long-ago beach, his desire, her *innocence*...

He shook off the useless thoughts and forced them back behind the firewalls of his conscience.

'All right, I'm sorry.' Even he could hear the gruffness in his voice. He resumed his stride, and evaded her gaze, a violent chaos in his heart. Guilt and remorse for what he'd done, the trouble he'd made for her, and, undermining his anger, a treacherous sort of tenderness. If he once looked into her eyes he wouldn't be able to resist touching her, holding her, and it could only lead to the pathway now forbidden for all eternity.

An honourable man did not seduce a woman, leave her pregnant, then seduce her all over again at the first opportunity. Especially after she'd rejected and dismissed him for the second time.

Regret speared through him for the passion he would never taste again. *Per carità*. What had he ever done to deserve this?

He noticed they'd turned off the route they'd come, down behind the shops and cafés and galleries, and had plunged into a maze of leafy little personal streets. He was insanely tempted all at once to take her hand, feel her slim palm in friction with his, but he controlled himself. That would be too much like affection. Affection was not what he could afford. She had made her embargoes clear. She didn't want him in her life. Not now, and never again.

They were passing what looked like a schoolyard, with painted swings and slides and childish paraphernalia. She turned her head, then paused as something inside the brick-and-iron fence caught her attention, causing him nearly to bump into her. The sudden proximity brought him an intoxicating whiff of her hair.

'Oh, look,' she said. 'Damn. See that? They've forgotten to cover the sandpit.'

'What?'

He hadn't meant to growl. It was probably the unwelcome realisation of what the place symbolised. Six years ago she'd never have paid the slightest attention to something as mundane as a schoolyard. He supposed mothers cared about such things.

His lip made an involuntary curl, and he decided for his sanity's sake to cull all thoughts of *the situation* from his mind. Concentrate on the here and now.

To make up for his impatience he made a polite display of peering into the dimly lit grounds with interest.

Across the playground, brick buildings loomed, grim and Victorian in the shadowy dark, lit by occasional security lights protruding from under their eaves. The yard looked ghostly, with shifting drifts of moonlight under big, spreading pines.

He followed her gaze and managed to determine a pale patch under the trees. Before he could make proper sense of it, she had lodged a toe onto the base of the fence, and was hoisting herself up onto the brick fence post. In another second she was down on the other side.

He had to admit, reluctantly swinging over after her a few resistant seconds later, she seemed as lithe and supple as she'd been six years before. No one would ever suspect she'd been swollen with child, as the saying went. The curve of her hips and long, slim legs still looked every bit as graceful in jeans. In fact, for a few seconds, when the feminine swell of her bottom had been deliciously defined as the fabric had tightened against her, he'd been reminded… Smooth and taut as a peach.

If only… If only his memory of seeing her nude weren't still so sharp.

She cast him a glance over her shoulder, alluring as sin while at the same time innocent, and it struck at his memory with an almost visceral bittersweet punch.

It was just the way she'd looked at him that faraway summer. Exactly the way.

'Here,' she said. 'Look.'

In a few strides he caught up and stood beside her, bemusedly gazing down at a large rectangular depression filled with sand. 'So?'

'It should have its cover on. I s'pose the janitor must have forgotten.' She glanced about her. 'I think I know where they keep it. I'll just run over and see if it's there.'

She turned and walked away in the direction of the buildings. As she receded from him and stepped into a pool of dark shadow her pale fall of hair remained a visible, beckoning gleam. Then she disappeared around a corner.

He took off after her, cursing, wishing it had all been different. As they had been before, without complications. Why did she have to bother with schoolyards? Why couldn't they just be lovers again, with the world on a string?

'It's around here,' she called. 'Do you mind giving me a hand?'

Perhaps it had been a mistake to kiss her in the brasserie. This was a *school*, hardly an erotic setting, but as he followed her into a shadowy alcove under a staircase in the deserted place the air suddenly sprang alive with sexual overtones. In spite of the taboo aspects of the occasion, echoes of rules and discipline and good behaviour, even worse, her now being a *mother*, that kiss simmered in his blood like a provocation.

Whatever she said, she couldn't deny her response to it. She'd wanted him.

'Oh, look, it's here.' She turned for an instant to glance at him, and the awareness in her eyes sparkled with as much promise and exhilaration as the bubbles in a fine prosecco. His heart rate quickened.

In the dull light cast by the security lamp he saw a wooden frame with a tarpaulin nailed across it, leaning against the rear wall.

She reached out to seize an end of it, then let it go at once with a little exclamation, sinking her teeth into her plump lower lip, then sucking at one of her fingers.

His blood stirred.

'Here,' he intervened, stepping forward to lift the modest frame from her, unavoidably brushing her with his body. Electricity thrilled through him, and he guessed she'd have felt the same little frisson.

'Careful of splinters.' There was huskiness in her voice, a sensual inflection she couldn't conceal.

He carried the frame easily across the asphalt to the grassy spot where the sandpit lay under the pines. 'You're very public spirited,' he observed. 'It's a fine night. Would it matter so much to have left it?'

She took the opposite end and helped to slide the cover into position. Then she straightened up, dusting her hands, wiping them on her shapely, denim-clad thighs, and gazed at him across the pit. In the moonlight her eyes were shadowy and unknowable, her face a pale heart shape.

'It keeps the cats out. Vivi plays in here with her friends.'

Vivi. The name seared his heart with a violent pang, but he ignored it and maintained his smooth expression.

Still, the name must have flared in there like an incendiary device, because somehow it sparked a wave of conflicting reactions. Regret was one of them, almost a savage, furious grief, and, underneath it all, the elusive old magic that had drawn him to Lara in the first place, now more potent than ever.

Sacramento, admit it. Desire.

Somehow in the hour since she'd informed him and shattered his peace of mind, she'd managed to acquire an added mystery, a primitive feminine power that attached to her being a mother. The mother of his—

He quickly suppressed that sentimental add-on. His *nothing*. His mistake.

Still, it had all created some upheaval inside him at a deep level. Despite his anger, the hurt, he felt possessed with a need to touch her, to make claim of her in the shadowy deserted schoolyard.

They stared at each other across a silence taut with vibrations.

Lust took a sweet ferocious hold of his loins, and against all reason he took a step towards her. A breeze stirred the pines and ruffled her pale hair, but she didn't move from her spot as he approached. She watched his advance around the children's playpit, her eyes glittering with awareness in her white face, her ripe mouth grave and expectant.

She was still too achingly beautiful. His beautiful, elusive torment.

'Lara,' he said thickly. 'Larissa…'

He seized her arms and pushed her back into the shadows, up against the trunk of a pine, and kissed her wine-sweet mouth fiercely. She didn't resist. Her soft lips delivered their own fiery response, and parted to invite him in. She raised her arms and linked them around his neck, and to his intense, grateful pleasure he felt her soft, pliant body yield to him in encouragement.

Like a starving man he covered her face and throat with his kisses, plundering her mouth with his lips and tongue until he was drunk with the taste and scent of her.

In this deserted, pine-scented place there was no watcher present to inhibit him. His hungry hands roamed free and bold, and he could have groaned with the pleasure of the feel of her curves under his palms. Her little sighs and moans, her erotic writhing drove him on to explore her pale body under her clothes, but he willed himself to maintain control, and firmly kept her hands from wandering.

He broke from her lips to swiftly unbutton her shirt. He heard her gasp as her bra was laid bare, and it spurred his passion for the glistening pale beauties swelling from the confining lace, their skin translucent in the frosty light. His mouth watered to taste them.

Her breath was coming in fast little trembling pants, her breasts heaving in voluptuous excitement.

Still possessing some degree of perspective of the place, he'd only intended to look, perhaps just once to *feel*, but her bra catch was set alluringly at the front. Barely before he was aware of what he was doing, the devil in him had unfastened the bra and allowed her breasts to spill into his hands.

Ah, that soft resilient flesh like no other. He kneaded them in his hands, then bent his head, unable to keep from kissing the scented skin. The taut nipples begged for his lips, and he tasted the delicate treasures one at a time, relishing their erotic stiffening in his mouth, his lust fanned by Lara's moaning responses.

He was almost unbearably hard now inside the constraints of his underwear, and the possibilities of plunging inside her slick heat for release began to assume a firmer reality. Aching for her nakedness, he slipped his fingers beneath the band of her jeans and felt for the button.

The yellow flare of a passing car's headlights swept the trees, and she froze in his arms. He covered her with his body, pleasurably tortured by the feel and fragrance of her, her face pressed into his neck, her heart thumping against his chest, the faint dew of moisture on her silken skin.

The lights disappeared, and he was ready to push her down onto the aromatic pine needles, but she stiffened in his arms.

'What are we doing?' she whispered hoarsely. 'This can't happen now. It can't happen.'

Disappointment surged through him. 'Ah, but you want me, *carissima*. Don't pretend.'

'It can't be like before, now, though, can it?' she said violently, then jerked away from him and started adjusting her clothes. 'We have to grow up.'

The unpalatable words lodged in his gut. 'Do you think there is any other way for us?' His voice echoed in the silent schoolyard, rough with unassuaged hunger.

He watched her tug the vest across her breasts and zip it, as though that might quell his passion for them, then he turned sharply away to wait for his pain to subside.

Too late, he could have told her. Far too late. For better or worse they had both crossed the line. There would be no going back.

The silent walk to her house was alive with a turmoil of unspoken communications. Passion simmered, unresolved, but it would find a way. Whatever she thought. Didn't she understand? This was what they were all about.

At her gate she paused, and bit her swollen lip. 'That

shouldn't have happened,' she said in a low, emotional voice. 'You're only in town for a few days. I can't just—be your—convenient woman.'

Despite his frustration and the dark chaos he was floundering in, he wanted to laugh. As if there had ever been anything convenient about Lara Meadows. Instead, though, he controlled himself and said gravely, 'Well, a lot can happen in a few days, *tesoro*.'

He heard her sharp intake of breath. She examined him with such obvious suspicion in her narrowed gaze he had to restrain himself from seizing her again. The temptation to steal another sweet, scorching taste of her lips was overwhelming, but he resisted. Leave her hungry. It would only fan his own flames, and God knew he needed to think.

A lamp shone over the porch, and there was a faint light glowing from the upstairs rooms. Despite his reluctance to tear himself away from her, he felt relieved she didn't invite him inside.

The truth was, he didn't care to look inside that sleeping house.

CHAPTER EIGHT

SLEEP was a long time coming to Alessandro, and when at last it did he dreamed it was summer, not the subtle, sometimes chill, showery summer he'd come from, but an Australian summer, with blazing blue skies and shimmering noonday heat. As it had been the day he'd flown in to fulfil his promise, with his great-grandmother's engagement ring burning a hole in his pocket.

He dreamed he was pursuing a woman down a leafy green lane, her hair floating out behind her like a cloud. Surely he'd dreamed this before. Then all at once it was dusk and the air was heavy with the fragrance of honeysuckle, and a poignant sense of longing. *His* longing, he realised, somehow standing outside himself in the dream.

The woman cast him a laughing glance over her shoulder, and he saw that it was Lara. Of course it was, who else? his outside self told him. He reached out to catch her, but just when he thought he had her, she slipped through his fingers, as elusive as a wraith. Then he realised with a sudden, gut-wrenching shock she was carrying a baby on her hip. He made a desperate effort to see the baby's face, but, however hard he tried, the child always turned its face away from him.

He woke at dawn with a start, his heart hammering, bathed in sweat and confusion, and an intense sense of loss that haunted him for hours.

The trouble was, he reflected while shaving, that, despite all his precautions to hold the situation at bay, hearing his child's name must have sparked something in his imagination. And if that hadn't been bad enough, try as he might not to acknowledge it, he couldn't completely eliminate an image of a small girl playing in that sandpit.

Later, showered and crisply shaven as he perused *The Sydney Morning Herald* over his coffee, it occurred to him that men had dealt with problems like this since the beginning of time. In Italy there'd have been no question that he should marry the woman at once. Her family would have demanded it, as would his own.

What his mother would say if she knew!

So what were his choices? Force an unwilling bride to the altar, or provide her with generous enough financial support that she could raise the child well on her own?

He wondered how much he could rely on what she'd said about the rules here. Certainly they didn't seem as clear-cut as they were at home. Women seemed able to live as single parents quite happily, without apparent social punishment.

Or did they? Perhaps he didn't know enough to interpret the subtleties woven beneath the easy-going surface of the Aussie way of life.

Anyway, a woman like Lara would almost certainly marry eventually. The only surprise was that some guy hadn't caught her already. There'd be one along soon, eager to marry her. Prepared to take on her child.

Alessandro's cup stilled in mid-air and stayed suspended there for moments, until he put it down. Replacing it, he must have used more force than he intended, for coffee splattered across the news page.

Passion shouldn't linger in the senses like a narcotic. A night of sleep should neutralise the effect, and allow a woman to start the new day with a fresh canvas.

Or perhaps that was how it was for normal people, Lara mused at the editorial meeting as she sat drinking in Alessandro's face.

Looked at in perspective, it hadn't been much more than a couple of kisses and a caress, but—*such* kisses, and such a caress. She supposed a woman who'd banished her dreams and applied herself to being a mother and a singleton must be more susceptible to after-effects. Like tossing and turning, and restlessness. And thinking and imagining, and fantasising. And worrying about whether she'd done the right thing on behalf of Vivi. Should she have tried to insist he take an active role, for Vivi's sake? Would she come to regret it later? Would Vivi?

But he was such an unpredictable force. Who'd have guessed he'd be exploding in wrath over the news one minute, then kissing her so passionately the next? This morning now, despite last night's shock, he looked calm and relaxed, though in some subtle way buzzing with purpose and energy. Amazing for a man who'd sustained a serious blow.

Glancing around at her colleagues, it was pretty clear that as he talked them through the new editorial guidelines hardly anyone was looking at their page. Their eyes were all glued to his face as if they were soaking him in through their pores. It wasn't too much of a stretch to guess that their tongues were near to hanging out.

The climate between boss and staff had warmed by at least a hundred degrees. Donatuila, on the other hand, while her occasional contributions were friendly, remained seated at her desk, twiddling a pencil in her hand while her watchful glance shifted from face to face.

Alessandro was deeply engaged in the task of charming the workforce. Lara had sensed the moment she walked in this morning that somehow yesterday's unrest seemed to have calmed.

It was hard to pinpoint exactly how he'd achieved it, for he was behaving like any other managing director—one with stunning dark eyes and a mouth made to drive a woman crazy, that was. Who could kiss like the devil. He was courteous, but autocratic in his subtle way, asking some diabolically pertinent questions that had people on their toes.

More than once his eyes left the page and drifted her way, and she felt as if her face were being exposed to a solar flare, although she tried not to let her extreme consciousness of last night's escapade in the schoolyard show.

The trouble was, it had provoked some unsettling dreams she could have done without. It did no good for a thirsty woman crawling through a desert on her hands and knees to dream of the taste of water.

Of drinking deeply. Plunging in. *Wallowing.*

Oh, she'd been so long in the desert. And she was only human, wasn't she? Having been given another taste of the overwhelming physical desirability of the man who'd given her a crash course in the A to Z of love, a man who was now *single* and *available*, how could she help but be awash with yearnings?

If only it hadn't been so complicated. Something told her that his response to the news might change when he'd had longer to process it. While her and Vivi's fates hung in the balance, it would be madness to become involved with him again. Who knew what he might persuade her into? Could she trust herself to be strong on Vivi's behalf?

Last night, gazing on Vivi's innocent sleeping face after she'd arrived home, she'd been shaken with her fear of what might happen if Alessandro decided he wanted his daughter. *Really* wanted her. Would he be content to visit her occasionally? Or would he expect a tiny little girl to be flown across the world to him for holidays, far from her mother's protection, nurturing and teaching? Or…

She felt a suffocating fear.

The Vincentis were a wealthy family. Alessandro could provide things for Vivi that Lara couldn't. What if he fought her for custody in the Australian courts, citing his wealth and the advantages he could offer? She dared not risk that. She *must* not.

She listened to his voice with barely half an ear, torn between wondering if seeing the results of the DNA test would make him feel differently, and trying not to dwell on the passion.

She had come so close last night to succumbing. Too close. She'd been so distracted, for a moment this morning she hadn't been able to remember if she'd slipped Vivi's lunch into her school bag.

'Excuse me, Mr Vincenti.' Kirsten leaned forward in her chair. 'How long did you say you and Ms Capelli would be with us?'

Alessandro swept them all with his dark gaze, then said quietly, 'I will be here until I am completely satisfied that everything is—exactly as it should be.'

Lara's pulse jumped up a notch. That wasn't what he'd said yesterday. Then it had been a simple matter of him sorting out the finances, appointing the new MD, then moving on to his next project.

The meeting ended. Lara rose with everyone else, and as she made for the door in their wake Alessandro called her back.

'Lara, will you stay a few minutes?' His eyes connected with hers and something hot and primitive shimmered in their dark depths. Her heart struck a couple of heavy gongs that reverberated through her insides, her mouth dried, and for a second she thought of the pine bark pressing into her back, his hands and mouth on her willing flesh.

She sensed Donatuila's sharp glance, and yanked herself together.

'Of course.' She tried to sound brisk and professional, but the memory of how it had been in his arms hummed in her blood like a witch's potion.

The door closed behind the others.

Alessandro's dark eyes flickered over her, and under her

clothes her skin cells tingled. He leaned casually on the edge of his desk, his sexy mouth edging up a little at the corners.

'I think you'll agree we need to talk properly. Last night things got a little—out of control. Perhaps we should meet in a less—tempting environment. How about we try for dinner this evening?'

She moistened her dry lips, thinking rapidly about the possible arrangements she could make for Vivi. 'Dinner. Well, I really shouldn't, not after last night.'

'After…?' he said politely. 'After making love to me in the schoolyard?'

She gasped. 'Oh, I did not…' She felt herself grow warm. 'I was only… It was *you*.' His brows lifted and she said quickly, 'No, please, don't apologise. I quite understand. It must have been the shock and everything.'

'It might have been the shock,' he agreed. 'Or then it might have been your charms. And the passion. My passion for you, your passion for me.'

'Oh, shh, shh.' Frowning, she shook her head, then, casting a quick look towards the door, lowered her voice. 'I wish you'd be serious. Don't you realise how serious this is for Vivi and me?'

His eyes glinted, then he lowered his lashes and said gently, 'Well, you know me, *tesoro*. I'm probably only concerned with how serious it is for me.'

'Oh.' Her blush swamped her from her toes to her scalp. 'I'm sorry. Truly. I know you wouldn't… I didn't mean to imply…'

'Of course you didn't. So, dinner then?'

How could she refuse? How many ways were there to offend a man in a twenty-four-hour period? 'Well…all right. I guess Mum won't mind, though I won't be able to stay late. I'll meet you somewhere. Where are you staying?'

He looked surprised. 'I'll pick you up.'

'No, no, that's all right. It's better that we meet in the city.'

'Why is that?' His eyes sharpened. 'You don't want me to come to your home?'

She hesitated. 'Well, you know you—you don't want to be involved with *the situation*. If Vivi sees you…'

She felt a sudden stillness in him, then he said easily, 'Surely she must have been introduced to men before.'

'Oh, well. Yes.' Her heart started to thump, and her hands to twist. 'Of course she has. My uncle, I s'pose, and husbands of my friends…a couple of the dads from the school… But, goodness—this wouldn't be like that. You're her *father*.'

'You wouldn't have to introduce me as that, though, would you?' She could feel his steady gaze on her face. 'You could say I was a friend.'

She widened her eyes. 'Alessandro, as soon as she heard your *name*…'

Something disturbed the cool surface of his dark irises. 'She knows my name?'

'Well, of course. You don't think I'd conceal the identity of her father from her, do you?'

He was silent, his lean, bronzed face as smooth and impenetrable as a wall. To fill the gap she said, her hands gesturing in appeal, 'It would be the most terrific shock for her. I'd have to prepare her, *talk* to her about it. She's only a little girl. A *baby*, really. She only really knows me, her grandma, her teacher at school… Her little friends, my girlfriends, Mum's and Dad's families.' She felt her throat thicken. 'It would be—quite a significant moment in her life. We couldn't just—spring it on her.'

He scanned her face with a veiled gaze, then shrugged. To her relief he said, 'I see. Well, then. We'd better meet in the city.' He slipped a mobile phone from his pocket and flipped it open. 'We should exchange numbers.'

She took out hers and he keyed in his number, while she did likewise.

He flicked a glance up at her. 'Shall we say the bar at the Seasons at seven?'

'Oh, the Seasons.' Her heart made a skittery little tremor, but she enquired with polite unconcern, 'So you're staying there?'

'Where else?' He smiled then, and his eyes gleamed like the devil's.

She turned for the door, then paused with her hand on the knob. 'This—won't be a date, Alessandro.'

'Won't it? What will it be, then?'

'*Well*. You know. It'll be—a meeting. Dinner between two adults.'

'Two adults,' he echoed musingly. 'Would that be two consenting adults, *tesoro*?'

'No, it would not,' she snapped. 'It would be two adults with a—a situation to resolve.'

As the door closed Alessandro's smile faded, and he turned to the window and stared down at the George Street traffic. He should have known when the Sydney takeover flashed up on the head office radar that Fate was somehow involved.

However he looked at it, whether she liked it or not, he was tied to Lara Meadows.

And her child.

He wondered idly who the child resembled. Probably took after her mother. It was to be hoped so, although surely he'd read that the dark-coloured gene was more likely to be dominant in determining eye colour. He would hardly be human not to be curious.

It would be a pity, if a man *happened* to have created a child, just one small soul among all the zillions that had ever existed, never to see its face.

Her face.

Lara tottered back to her desk and collapsed in her chair to plan what she would wear. Not that it was important. She wasn't trying to beguile him, or anything. There was no point, if he was flying back to the other side of the world in the not too distant future.

Of course, if there'd been any possibility of him staying she might have considered having another shot at it. He still seemed very attracted, while *she*... And he was gorgeous, he made her heart race like a mad thing, and— She put her hands to her face.

He was the father of her child.

Funny how last night he hadn't wanted to hear a thing about Vivi, while today...

Today she could have sworn he'd listened closely to everything she said.

CHAPTER NINE

FIVE o'clock took an eternity to arrive. Lara was first out the door, knowing she had to run for the early train home, see Vivi settled with Greta, try to make herself gorgeous, and rush back into town.

She only hoped her little black dress would be good enough. She'd loved it when she bought it for the staff dinner, but the woman Alessandro had chosen to marry, be it ever so briefly, was a fashionista of the first order. How could she compete with that? Single mothers couldn't afford Milano dresses, and a man of his sophistication would be sure to realise her dress's lack of pedigree.

But there wasn't much choice. It was either the black or a tea-dress she'd worn to a wedding the year before.

She made an impatient gesture at herself. How pathetic she'd become, worrying about this kind of detail when six years ago she'd hardly given a thought as to whether Alessandro admired her clothes. It had been enough then that he'd appreciated her in whatever she wore.

Well, seemed to. Last night had certainly felt like appreciation. The trouble was, it had knocked her completely off-balance. How had a tense, serious situation reignited such smouldering passion? And there was no use blaming Alessandro. In her heart she had to acknowledge she'd been equally aroused. Perhaps, on his side, it was just the inevitable hangover from the past, but on her side the sweet old painful feelings lingered on. Trouble was, heartbreak was wrapped up with them now.

Still, somehow her emotions had to be put aside for Vivi's sake. Whatever happened tonight, she couldn't forget its significance for Vivi's future.

Later, though, surveying herself in her black lacy bra, undies, and sheer, silky stay-up stockings, in spite of her resolutions her excitement jumped a notch. They looked *right*, as if the real Lara Meadows, the sexy, feminine Lara, who wasn't afraid to be frivolous with clothes, had been called up and given a last brief chance at life.

Vivi looked on with big, solemn eyes as she paraded herself in front of the mirror, only just restraining herself from giving her hips a wiggle.

The babe was *back*.

She slipped on the dress. It was a dramatic sheath that fell to just above her knees, with a simple but stunning reliance on her curves for shape. The sleeves were elbow length, and, though it wasn't a wild plunger, the bodice dipped to reveal a generous glimpse of cleavage. At least she *had* a cleavage now, thanks to her darling.

She hardly ever wore earrings for fear of drawing attention to the scar tissue that travelled from behind her ear, down her nape almost to her shoulder, but the dress demanded them. After a quick search she fastened in some pearls that nestled in her lobes. Hair swinging halfway to her waist, stockings, stiletto heels, eyeshadow, red lipstick… She should pass, shouldn't she?

Saying her goodbyes to Vivi in the kitchen where Greta was preparing dinner, she tried to act as if it were any other evening out and she weren't stirred up with an excitement that bordered on fever.

'And don't worry, Mum. I'll make sure I'm back before eleven. You'll have plenty of time to make your shift.'

As she let Vivi slide to the floor Greta said casually, 'Do you think he might change his mind?'

Lara restrained herself from glancing down at Vivi. For a second she held her breath. 'I don't know. Last night—I wouldn't have thought so. Today—I can't predict.' She met Greta's all-too-perceptive eyes. 'I know, I know. But Venice is a long way from here, Mum. Think of that.'

And she had to remember what tonight was all about, she thought, slipping on her black coat. She really needed to cool it. Trouble was, it was overwhelmingly clear to her now that she'd only been half alive for the past six years. It was impossible not to look forward to seeing him, to relish meeting him at the Seasons just like before, fired up with the old anticipation that felt so much like joy.

If only she remembered to keep control of herself, stick to the script and not—*not*—agree to go upstairs to his room.

As she closed the front door behind her she noticed a sleek black limousine parked across from the house, dominating the smaller cars parked along the narrow street with its size. Heavens. One of those air hosties had landed a big one.

As she reached the gate the driver got out and, to her bemusement, started crossing the street to her. When he reached the footpath on her side he said, with a respectful tilt of his cap, 'Miss Meadows?'

Oh, God.

Alessandro stepped from the lift and strolled across to the bar. He was early, but he wanted to catch sight of Lara first. He chose a stool at one end that gave him a strategic view of the entrance.

The bartender glanced at him, but Alessandro shook his head. Not yet. He needed a clear brain.

He glanced at his watch, musing on times he'd met her here before. She'd rush through those glass doors, all lit up as if switched on with some internal glow. It had seemed to him that she stood out in any crowd—he'd always been certain other men must notice her and would try to win her away from him. At that time he'd seemed to possess some magic faculty that had helped him to sense her presence in a room, even before he'd actually seen her.

As if to taunt him, something drew his gaze to the door, and held it fast while his pulse jumped. She was there, paused inside the entrance, taking her bearings and unbuttoning a black coat that came to her mid-calf, somehow emphasising the slenderness of her legs and fine slim ankles.

He was aware of that rare sensation in his chest.

She caught sight of the bar and started to make for it, the chandeliers catching the gloss of her hair, expectation in her face. After last night, he was noticing the changes in her. She wasn't the giddy girl she'd been when he first knew her, always rushing, bubbling over with exuberance. He could see now she walked with a graceful, womanly glide, the confidence of maturity in her steady gaze.

But she still had the glow, he recognised with a quickening of his blood, seeing her search for him, her eyes bright, lips ever so slightly parted. That heart-stopping glow.

Their gazes connected, and his pulse jumped. He strolled to meet her, controlling an urge to run across and catch her up in his arms.

'Hello.'

He embraced her and bent to brush her cheeks with his lips. They were cold, nipped to rosiness by the wind even in the transition from the limo to indoors, but the fragrance of her skin and hair rose in his nostrils like an intoxication.

With last night hot in his blood, he felt the irresistible stir in his loins. She was wearing something black under the coat, with a neck-line that revealed an alluring hint of her breasts. Her eyes were as seductive, with shadow on their lids, her luscious mouth a rich deep red. Their gazes connected only fleetingly, but long enough for him to see the feverish little sparkle. The buzz in his veins escalated. Whatever she said, this was a long way from a mere meeting.

She spoke very rapidly, slightly breathless, the way she always had when her excitement was on the simmer.

'That was extremely nice of you to send the limo. I hardly know what to say.' She made a gesture as though to touch him, but her hands fluttered in the air then drew back without making contact. 'Thank you so much. It was lovely and warm, though, honestly, there wasn't the least need.' She smiled. 'I only hope the neighbours were watching.'

He smiled too, conscious of the spark in his own blood. 'The least I could do, since your home is off-limits. For the moment, at least.' She looked quickly at him, but he only smiled and with a tilt of his head indicated the bar. 'Would you care for a drink before dinner?'

'Oh…er…do you mind if we order dinner somewhere more or less straight away? I can't stay too late.' She glanced at her watch. 'I promised Mum I'd be back by ten thirty. She has to work later. I can't leave—her alone.'

Her. No, of course not. Though this certainly curtailed the possibilities. Unless…

Well, *Dio mio,* how he loved a challenge.

He kept his expression grave. 'That's a pity. We'll just have to see what we can fit in between now and ten-thirty. Would you prefer to stay here where it's warm, or walk down the street to one of the restaurants?'

She hesitated and glanced about, and he watched the indecision flit across her face. Whether to dine here, with his bed calling from upstairs, or to brave walking out into the cold with nothing to protect her legs from the wind except that faint Lycra shimmer?

She met his eyes, a small determined gleam in hers. 'I think—down the street.'

'Ah,' he said, amused. Did she really think she could outmanoeuvre Alessandro Vincenti? 'I thought you'd say that. I booked us a table at one of the places around the corner.'

She started buttoning up again, and he took charge of the top two buttons, enjoying the conscious flutter of her lashes, knowing how intimate the gesture was, how tempted she was to look up into his eyes. Then he took her arm—purely a friendly gesture, surely. When the glass entrance doors opened before them, they were met by new arrivals coming in, a perfect reason to slide his arm around her waist to steady her against his body.

Even through the layers of her clothing his fingers thrilled to the response in her vibrant flesh, and it stirred his blood like no aphrodisiac ever could.

When he released her outside, the all too brief, tantalising touch stayed with him, and he'd have been willing to bet his billion dollar share in Scala Enterprises that her slim, supple body felt the same yearning loss.

Nothing *like* a meeting.

He signalled the valet to summon a taxi. The distance wasn't great. If the evening had been warmer the walk past all the boutiques, tourist shops and historic byways of this old section of the city would have been pleasant, but his aim was to warm her up, not chill her down.

CHAPTER TEN

THE restaurant was an old converted terrace house, charmingly furnished with antiques, its floorboards slightly uneven, but to Lara's relief it was warm, courtesy of a combustion stove in the crowded front room. A jazz quartet occupied one corner, and while her ear responded to a sultry rendition of 'The Man I Love' her mouth watered at the tantalising aromas issuing from the kitchen.

Her pleasure in those old dining experiences with Alessandro came rushing back. How he'd adored restaurants, and she'd plunged into his enthusiasm with him. Food was of the most immediate importance, he'd once sternly told her, shocked by her cavalier attitude to what she ate. She'd felt so sophisticated, dining with a connoisseur of fine food and wine. She remembered how easy and casual he'd always been then, how generous to staff.

The waiter led them through several packed rooms to a table in a smaller room beyond, where Alessandro had to duck his head to avoid the lintel. Two other tables in the room were unoccupied. After a second Lara realised there were no place settings on those other tables.

She glanced quickly at Alessandro, looking so darkly handsome and assured in his elegant suit. Her knees had only just started to recover from the sight of him strolling towards her at the Seasons. Would the Marquis of the Isles have arranged for them to have this private little dining room all to themselves?

She slipped off her coat and handed it to the waiter. She could feel Alessandro's gaze and turned to see him assessing her in her black dress. The wolfish hunger in his eyes thrilled through her with a delicious awareness of her femininity. She'd almost forgotten the sensation of being desired by a gorgeous man, of feeling beautiful and sexy and fascinating.

Oh, Lord. How had she survived for so long without it? Without *him*?

His dinner setting had been placed adjacent to hers, and as he took his chair she absorbed the graceful old-fashioned furnishings, long lace-edged linen cloths, tall windows draped in long swathes of blue satin. A chaise longue set against one wall extended a silent, though potent, invitation.

'This is very intimate,' she said with a smiling lift of her brows once the waiter had delivered their menus and departed. 'Perfect for a serious discussion, isn't it?'

His eyes gleamed, then flickered down to where her bodice dipped to the valley between her breasts. 'And we have a lot to talk about, don't we, *tesoro*?' He flashed her a devil's smile, then opened the wine list and started to study it.

'Something to start? A cocktail, perhaps?' She nodded and satisfaction settled in the chiselled lines of his sexy mouth. 'Good. Something to warm you up. Let's see now…you like strawberry…a Strawberry Kiss?' His brows edged together as he perused the list. 'No, too icy. We can do better than that. How about a Between the Sheets? Or perhaps a French 69? A little gin, some champagne…'

'I think I'd prefer mine straight, thank you. Just straight old-fashioned champagne.'

His sensuous lips gave a very faint twitch. 'Straight up it will be. Though we'd better be careful,' he murmured, returning to the list. 'I don't want to get you drunk. Not now you're a mother.'

She smiled and raised her brows, pleasantly stimulated by

the delicious little bout of sexual innuendo. 'Can't mothers enjoy themselves?'

'I've been led to believe that mothers can be very puritanical.'

'That isn't always the case. I think it might depend on who the mothers are with.'

'Ah.' He flicked her a smiling glance. After a moment his eyes veiled and he said, 'How is—what did you call her? Vivi?'

Her heart skipped up a gear but she smiled and she gave a wary nod. 'That's right. Short for Vivienne. She's—fine. She should be in bed round about now. Grandma will be reading her a story.'

'She has another grandmother, you know,' he said absently, scrutinising his menu. 'I'm guessing you'll order the pumpkin soup. Yes?'

Her heart made an alarmed lurch, and it wasn't inspired by his amazing recall of her passion for pumpkin soup.

'Does she?' The words sounded as if they'd been through a strainer, courtesy of a sudden blockage in her larynx. It was probably caused by her daunting vision of an elegant Italian woman swanning across the marble floors of a *palazzo* with frescoed walls. The dowager Marchesa of the Venetian Isles, matriarch of a rich and powerful family. A family with a strong sense of commitment to possessing what was theirs.

'Don't look so alarmed, *carissa*.' His eyes glinted. 'I'm not a clairvoyant, just a guy with a very good memory.'

She collected herself, and managed a smile. 'I'm *immensely* flattered.'

The waiter came back to assure Alessandro that the fish had been swimming in the sea no longer than two hours prior to this moment. The young man whisked away with their orders, then bustled back with champagne and tall flutes, removed the cork from the bottle and poured them each a glass.

After they'd clinked glasses and tasted the effervescent nectar, Alessandro said, 'I have spoken to my lawyers today. As soon as you provide your banking details funds will be deposited into your account.'

She flushed, frowning. 'Oh, do we have to talk about money? I never intended... This is not about that.'

'Whether you like it or not, it has to be about that, Lara.' His eyes were all at once cool and steady, like a man who would brook no opposition.

'But—' It was painful, but she had to say it. 'Surely you will want to see the DNA evidence before you take any steps. I've looked it up on the Internet. There are plenty of local labs who will do it for us without you having to be—personally involved with—with Vivi. They send you a kit.'

Alessandro watched her slim hands clench and unclench. She was afraid, that much was clear. Afraid of his involvement with her child. Hoping he would disappear from the scene.

He said quietly, 'Do you think I won't believe your word?'

Lara stared down into her glass, then looked up. 'I think it's best if we—do everything by the book. In years to come when you're settled down with your next wife and—other children in Venice, London, New York or wherever, I would not like you to have any doubts.'

He gazed silently at her, his dark eyes unreadable, then said softly, 'And where will you be then, *tesoro*? In those years to come?'

She smiled and said brightly, 'Oh, here of course. With my gorgeous girl.'

'What? No husband? You won't be looking for one?'

She heard his subtle mockery and maintained the smile even though she could feel heat rise through her neck and her cheeks. What was he doing? Torturing her with the forbidden subject? The truth was, that nerve he'd touched was so rarely acknowledged it was quite excruciatingly tender. But she'd die before she'd admit it to anyone, least of all him.

'Who knows?' She gave her shoulders an airy lift, and lifted her glass to her lips. 'I might still find one.'

He lounged back in his chair and stretched out his long legs, a sensual smile lurking in his dark eyes. 'Yeah. There was that guy who liked you. What was his name? Bill?'

'Bill who?' She frowned queryingly.

'Bill. Your MD.'

'Oh, *Bill*.' In spite of her discomfort she broke into a laugh, thinking of poor Bill, with his wife of twenty years and brood of unruly children. 'Yes, yes, he's a definite possibility.' She frowned and tilted her head in mock consideration. 'All right, Sandro, you've talked me into it. I'll marry Bill. Get him on the phone. Ask him if he likes kids.'

His thick black brows twitched. 'If you take my advice you won't jump into anything. I did that once and it was a shocking mistake.' He reached out and took one of her hands. 'But I'm glad to have this chance to be with you before you settle down with some guy, *tesoro*.'

She smiled, though it cost her an effort. The backs of her eyes were dangerously close to pricking and her poor stupid heart was being squeezed in a vice. She said a little hoarsely, 'And I must say *I'm* glad to have caught you between marriages.'

He leaned over and kissed her lips. Just a gentle little sexy kiss, but it was enough to reignite last night's wildfire, and send her blood coursing to her breasts.

It was only a gentle taunt, but so confusing. Why couldn't he be serious? Whatever happened to the Italian belief that marriage was an imperative for women with children?

Their first courses arrived. Her soup was rich and fragrant, delicately spiced with nutmeg, perhaps a trace of ginger, with tiny green flecks of spinach floating in it.

In between mouthfuls she did her best to steer the conversation into useful channels. His work kept him in London for the moment, he told her, though he'd spent time in Zurich, Stockholm and Brussels, and had lived in New York for a couple of years. Not a good lifestyle for a parent. Or a husband, come to that.

'Do you enjoy this work for the company? Never settling in one place?'

He shrugged, and heaped some of his abalone salad onto his fork. 'It's the work I've chosen.'

'And is that…?' She probably wouldn't have asked if she hadn't finished her champagne and been halfway through the Margaret River blanc. But beneath her flirty surface, questions were boiling up in her, things she had to know, even if they cut her to ribbons.

She raised her eyes to his. 'Is that why your marriage didn't work? All the travelling you do?'

He was still a second, his face impassive. Then he said coolly, 'It didn't continue because of a lack of passion.'

'Oh.' She flushed. 'Then why—?' She stopped herself in time. For heaven's sake, did she want him to think she cared? In fact, she didn't want to know anything about how they'd been together. It was ages ago now, anyway, ancient history. Still, she couldn't prevent herself from reaching one step further, even though she realised she was advancing into dangerous territory. His razor sharp brain could pick up any veiled intention, however carefully she concealed it.

She took a casual sip of her wine, met his sharp gaze, then quickly glanced away. 'So…you and Giulia didn't consider having children?'

The thick black brows made a twitch, then he lowered his lashes, shaking his head at some private irony. 'Never.'

'Was that because you—you didn't want children, or Giulia didn't?'

He gave an amused shrug, but his eyes were glinting in that alert way that warned her to take care. 'Does any man *want* children, *tesoro*? Men want women, and they move heaven and earth to win the ones they desire. Children are the inevitable baggage that goes along with them. Most men accept the price if the prize is worth it.' He smiled, and it crept into his eyes and made tiny little charm lines fan out from the corners. 'So I'm told.'

She returned the smile, but her insides plunged into a seething chaos.

So he'd put up with children if he wanted the mother enough, would he? For the sake of passion with the object of his desire, that woman he'd move heaven and earth for.

She wasn't the jealous type, but those words throbbed like a stab-wound. She was afraid of the outcome if he should *want* Vivi, but she realised all at once she couldn't bear him to *not* want her. Obviously she didn't want him to take her baby away, but what if Vivi needed him some time?

And she was bound to. Call it the wine, or the music, but now he was here in the flesh, the gorgeous, irresistible flesh, the truth was shouting at her from every angle. Greta was absolutely right. Vivi needed her father.

Maybe she shouldn't have let him off the marriage hook so easily. Did he seriously think she should look for some other man? Some *imposter*?

If he was basing his advice on his own experience, then she didn't think much of it. Certainly, he might have gone to extraordinary lengths to win Giulia. But if he'd wanted the beautiful socialite so much, how could he then have dallied in Sydney, making love to *her*?

It made her wonder, though. Why hadn't their passion lasted? Had they burned themselves out? Had he been so *hot* for Giulia, hotter than he'd been for her? How was that even possible?

She was torturing herself with the images just as the waiter glided in bearing their next courses.

When they'd been served she watched Alessandro speak to the young man with the charming civility that always made people twist themselves inside out to fulfil his lightest whim. The boy floated away, a glow in his eyes, ready to juggle plates on his head if it would make the Italian man's dining experience the richer.

Six years ago, she'd been one of those people. Perhaps that had been her downfall. She'd been so unsophisticated, she'd had no skill in subterfuge, no way of concealing how overwhelmed she was. How deeply she'd fallen.

And she could see that Giulia was the sort of woman men would regard as a prize. She had that lush Mediterranean beauty, she was glam and glitzy and socially connected. From what Lara had gleaned, she was the sort to be found in the thick of the celeb crowd, the Milano fashion week, ski-ing at San Moritz. Perhaps she was one of those flirty *signorinas* who laughed a lot in a vivacious, sexy way and played an elusive game that drove natural-born hunters like Alessandro mad with lust.

Whatever the reason for the marriage's failure, one depressing truth lingered on, in Lara's mind at least.

She stared down at her chargrilled baby snapper, balancing on its elegant little plinth of asparagus. Even when she'd been fresh and unspoilt at twenty-one, good in a bikini, with the bloom of youth in her cheek—at her peak, some might have said—she'd still been no match for the prize that glittered from Italy.

'Salad?'

She looked up and met Alessandro's faint, questioning smile.

'Please.' She allowed him to help her to some pretty coloured leaves masquerading as lettuce. She said in a casual, conversational tone, 'I saw some pictures of your wedding in a magazine once while I was waiting in a doctor's surgery. Giulia is a very beautiful woman.'

The salad servers halted infinitesimally on their way back to the bowl. Alessandro's black lashes momentarily screened his eyes, then flicked up to reveal a gaze darker and more fathomless than the most inaccessible chasm in the Bindinong Range.

He took time, as if choosing his words very carefully. 'I

didn't marry her for the usual reasons. It was not something I planned.' She gave him time to expand on his answer, gazing expectantly at him, and he said at last, a faint exasperation in his voice, 'It was a marriage of convenience. Almost at once it became very *in*convenient. It was annulled even before all the wedding gifts had been opened.'

'Annulled!' Her eyes widened.

Alert to the minefield he was traversing, Alessandro watched her process the implications, concealing his surge of sardonic amusement. Did it make his marriage less of a crime if there'd been no sex? He made a small grimace. If a woman rejected a man, for whatever reasons, why should she resent his finding solace elsewhere?

'The reason for it disappeared.' He sank his fork into the tender flesh of his blue-eyed cod with bland unconcern. 'There was no point. So we put an end to it.'

After a second he flicked her a glance and noticed a very faint wrinkling of her brow as she weighed up the possibilities of *him*, Alessandro Vincenti, contracting a marriage and not engaging in sex. He'd have laughed himself if that raw nerve hadn't recently been exposed to the elements. Who'd have believed that the events of six years past could still destabilise a man's serenity?

'Alessandro…' She extended a hand to touch his. 'I know men never want to admit this, but—did Giulia—*hurt* you?'

Disconcertingly, he saw something like compassion in her blue gaze.

He managed not to choke and stared at her in outraged incredulity. It took all of his control not to grab her and shake her. Was it possible she was thinking…? What, that his *virility* was in question?

He made a curt gesture with his fork. 'There was no hurt involved. It was a mutual arrangement, without emotion of any sort.'

'Oh, right.' She nodded, but it was clear she understood

nothing. *Per carità*. Did she seriously believe he was the sort of man who could love a woman, then five minutes later fall in love with another?

He exhaled a long breath. This was going to be harder than he'd ever imagined possible. He lounged negligently back in his chair and stretched out his long legs, his long tanned fingers curled loosely around the stem of his glass. 'You're frowning, *tesoro*. You're not worrying about Vivi?'

'Not at all. She's with my mother. I know she's in safe hands.'

'Ah, yes. She seemed like a very safe mother. Will *she* be worried about *you* now, that is the question.'

Lara smiled. He didn't know the half of it. 'Why would she be?'

'Well, mothers want their daughters to stay on the straight and narrow, I find. If she suspected her daughter of being in the hands of a big bad wolf who was planning to eat her up…'

Her sexual receptors swung to attention, and a pang of the old excitement zinged through her. Aha. This was a game she could enjoy.

She gave him a cool glance across the rim of her glass and fluttered her lashes. 'My mother knows I can keep big bad wolves at bay.'

'Are you sure you want to?'

The sensual golden shimmer in his hot dark eyes kindled something deep in her womb and ignited her nipples with a warm, restless yearning inside her lacy black bra.

Temptation caught her in its velvet claws. She'd resolved not to succumb again, but was that strictly necessary? Trouble was, last night was still so fresh in her senses. Surely, for old times' sake, big girls could separate sex from love?

She said softly, 'I'll have to think.'

She gave him a long look from beneath her lashes, then turned her attention to her fish, taking her time to relish the tender flesh and piquant sauce. The challenge pulsed between them, stirring a yearning in her veins and an anticipatory tingle in her erotic regions.

Her lips closed over a succulent morsel on her fork. Feeling his hot gaze, she cast him a soft glance, her eyes just meeting his smiling, sensual look without quite lingering.

Eventually her fish's delicate little spine was laid bare, and for a tiny instant she allowed her eyes to collide fully with his dark, shimmering gaze. At once she was flooded with the vision of how it had felt locked in his embrace, heart to thundering heart, and a wave of longing trapped the breath in her throat.

'So?' His voice was as dark and smoky as Satan's.

Hers was so husky it seemed to come from deep in her diaphragm. 'I know what would be the wise course.'

The strong lean hands wielding knife and fork arrested, and a flame blazed momentarily in his eyes' dark depths, startling her with the wild notion that there was more than mere desire smouldering in him, but something as fierce as molten lava.

'Haven't you learned yet, Larissa?' He spoke so forcefully the ghost of old Venice whispered through the polished patina of his perfect English. 'In some matters there's of no use to be *wise*.' He pounded the table with his fist, making the silver jump. 'There are moments in your life that you need to seize with both your hands.'

She stared at him in shock, her heart thudding at some veiled comprehension she couldn't quite read. Was he talking about six years ago?

'Well…well, how do I know this is one of them?'

He touched his linen napkin to his lips, then threw it down and sprang to his feet. Before she even had time to react he seized her and dragged her up out of her chair, thundering, 'This is *how*.'

He pulled her into his arms and brought his stern, chiselled mouth down on hers with such fierce hunger that after the first stunned instant her lips ignited with a fiery demand of their own. She responded to the fabulous pressure, thrilled by the feel of his lean solidity, hard against her breasts and thighs. As his marauding tongue tantalised the silken walls of her mouth, the flavours of raspberry vinaigrette, wine, and big, sexy man rose in her senses and intoxicated her entire being.

Her bones dissolved.

Oh, *God*. Ravished in a public restaurant.

Lucky he was holding her. Lucky…? His every touch resonated through her like the deep vibrant chords of a double bass.

And as if he too were trapped by the electric connection, like a ravenous wolfhound he dragged her even closer to him, his big lean frame in arousing friction with her curves. She thrilled to the feel of him, sliding her hands under his jacket to explore the powerful muscled body radiating heat through his shirt.

He deepened the kiss and her hot, feverish blood rushed to inflame her nipples. With a moan she raised her arms to link around his neck, caressing his nape and clutching at his thick black hair.

Please, please, yearned her breasts, and other erotic places. In total oblivion of the surroundings, her wanton flesh tingled to his caressing hands on her arms, ribs and hips, every skin cell silently longing, *begging* for those delicious hands to move into more dynamic territory.

To urge him on she writhed a little against his muscled frame, and was rewarded to feel a hard convincing prod against her abdomen, at the same time as his hand slid to her breast and closed around it in a thrilling hold.

'…me. Er…sir. Excuse me, sir, madam. If you wouldn't…'

An irritating, wispy little buzz-fly in her ear solidified itself in her consciousness as a human voice, and she wrenched herself from the escalating delights and sprang guiltily from Alessandro's grasp.

Trembly with arousal, she took a much-needed drag of air, and made some hurried adjustments to her dress.

The waiter, his boyish shiny face tinged with pink, stood

with his gaze fixed on the wall, menus clutched to his chest. Through a hot flustered haze she saw beyond him to the neighbouring table, where two couples were now being seated, casting sly smirking looks their way.

She risked a glance at Alessandro, and wished she hadn't. He was devouring her with his eyes, looking as famished as a wild beast, and she felt her flush deepen.

'Sir… Would—would s-sir and madam care for a dessert?'

She noted Alessandro snap from his contemplation of her and turn away, glancing thoughtfully around at the architecture while running a nonchalant hand through his hair. He responded to the lad with almost his usual poise, though his deep voice had developed a flattering hoarseness.

'Give us ten, twenty minutes to think about it.' He exchanged a narrow, man-of-the-world glance with the boy and the lad responded to it with a knowing nod. Then, as coolly as if nothing unusual had happened, Alessandro held her chair for her, before resuming his own place.

The boy presented them with their menus and departed at high speed.

Still embarrassed, and hyper-conscious of their neighbours, especially the women, who could hardly keep their eyes off Alessandro, though now he was angled away from them they couldn't catch more than an occasional stunning profile, Lara leaned over and whispered, 'I think we should go now.'

'Ah,' he said silkily, his eyes lighting, 'but where? Where should we go, *tesoro*?'

'Well…home, I suppose.'

'Your place?'

'*God*, no.' She felt his hand come to rest on her knee under the table, and her heart rocked into a dance number. 'I mean, that is…'

Under stress, her brain cells were capable of some pretty rapid calculation. Her place was out of the question. But, though time was running out, she was having such a good time, all stirred up like a flesh-and-blood woman for the first time in years. Home would have been such a tame end to things.

Alessandro began an absent-minded, gentle stroking motion along her leg. It might have been comforting, if it hadn't been so arousing. She struggled with herself to pull away, but her limbs were still heavy with the intoxication of the kiss.

'Perhaps,' she said, panting a little, hardly daring to meet his eyes for fear of alerting him to what his supple fingers were absent-mindedly doing, and breaking the fabulous connection, 'perhaps we could have—dessert at your hotel.'

He didn't smile, exactly, but satisfaction settled into the lines of his sensuous, chiselled mouth.

She was so grateful for long linen tablecloths. More places should have them, she thought. Especially when, to her absolute shameless pleasure, his fingers slipped under her dress and to the inside of her leg, and traversed her silky stocking all the way to the top.

'Although,' he said, holding his menu in his other hand to peruse, 'it says here that they have wild strawberries with dark drizzling chocolate. Couldn't we enjoy drizzling our wild strawberries with chocolate?'

That bare skin at the top of her stockings was even silkier than the stocking, and Alessandro's fingers seemed to know that and adapt accordingly. Absent or not, his very fingertips acquired a magic touch that roused her skin cells to heights of delight, inside her thigh, nearly all the way up to the elastic edge of her pants.

Inside the flimsy fabric, skin cells yearned in burning anticipation for their turn at the magic fingers. How high would those clever, artful fingers go?

She noticed a slight beading of sweat appear on Alessandro's upper lip.

'Oh, oh, perhaps…' She managed to sit perfectly still, though she parted her thighs a little further to give greater access and her breathing started to come in short quick gasps.

With her breasts rising and falling like an abducted maiden's in a sheikh film, her voice had a husky, breathless quality, brought about by trembling, pleasurable suspense. 'Perhaps strawberries in sauce can be a little messy. With—the strawberries being so—so juicy, and all…'

'Oh, no, *carissima*,' he said in his most velvet voice, gazing at her with grave assurance. 'I am sure nothing—well, hardly anything—could be tastier. What's a little juice?'

Hypnotised, she felt his soft fingers trail across the fabric of her pants, every subtle stroke delivering shock waves of delicious, tingling pleasure to the yearning delta beneath.

'Sorry, what was that you said?' He was teasing her, wicked laughter in his eyes, knowing her difficulty in speaking while swooning with the forbidden ecstasy.

'Oh,' she gasped, 'I mean, yes, yes, Alessandro, Alessandro…'

The waiter hovered into view, to her intense regret, and Alessandro swiftly removed his sinful hand, leaving her in a severely aroused and unresolved state while attempting to appear like a model citizen, and not to pant.

The boy stood by their table once more, and Alessandro smiled charmingly at him and said, 'You know, I don't think we'll stay for dessert after all.'

Outside in the small foyer as she buttoned up her coat, Alessandro said, 'The taxi shouldn't be long.'

'Can't we just walk? I don't want to stay here another *second*.'

'Oh.' He looked rueful. 'And I thought you were enjoying yourself.' She glowered at him, and he added, 'I don't want you to get cold. I was shocked by how thin that dress is. I could feel everything through it, every curve, every little hill and valley.'

She said repressively, 'I *need* to be cold.'

He laughed, and she pushed open the street door and threw him a stern glance.

'Are you coming?'

Outside, her face registered the blessed chill, but despite her brisk tone there was a bubbly exhilaration in her blood that had an insulating effect against the night air. It had been so long since she'd been seduced by a gorgeously sexy man with smiling eyes and no morals. Still, did that mean she should allow herself to plunge enthusiastically back into being his wanton plaything?

A shameless part of her was almost inclined to think it did. Having gone so far…with nothing resolved…

For God's sake, though, even if *he* didn't, she had principles, and responsibilities, and loyalties that came first. And then there was the time element. It was well after nine, and she needed to be home early enough for her mother to make her hospital shift.

Despite the chill night there were people strolling around the streets, gangs of tourists taking snaps of each other, spilling from the crowded cafés. Didn't Sydney people ever stay at home?

She shouldn't, she knew, lose sight of the fact that she'd aged. Twenty-one was a million years from twenty-seven, in terms of smoothness, slenderness and muscle tone. Certainly she was still slim, but it was a different sort of slim at twenty-seven. It was the slimness achieved from washing, cleaning, ironing, bending to pick up toys, staying constantly alert to the whereabouts of a small dynamo, and running, running, running.

Would he notice the difference?

She walked quickly, his long stride keeping easy pace with hers. Their words hung in the air in little drifts of vapour. She made an earnest attempt to chat about neutral, non-inflammatory things—the unusually hard winter, the boutiques and lighted shop windows they passed, occasional alluring little laneways and their fascinating old houses. She even seized one promising moment when they passed a children's book-shop for some deep probing into his attitudes about early childhood education, but instead of looking at the books, his dark sensual gaze remained on her.

In fact, it would be true to say that every conversational gambit she tried evoked an amused glance from Alessandro, while inside she was a turbulent sea of indecision.

With every second that passed she could sense the deepening vibration of sexual inevitability. Every shimmering glance from his dark eyes reflected the fever she felt churning through her own veins. That kiss and its sexy little aftermath had started a fire that could turn into a forest blaze at any tick of the clock. And if her recent compliance was anything to go by, she was unlikely to have much power of resistance.

She'd resolved not to go to his room, and where was she headed at this very moment, if not the suite at the Seasons? Perhaps, if he didn't touch her, she'd cool down and summon up the resistance to catch the train home.

After a few minutes he said, 'Slow down a little, *carissa*. Enjoy the crisp night.'

She shrugged and slowed her steps. Smiling, he held out his hand to her and what was she to do? It would have taken a stronger woman than her to resist the invitation in those dark eyes. She allowed him to clasp her hand in his strong grasp. She might have been weak, but it felt so pleasant, that electric connection with his warm, hard palm, as if she were all at once tuned into the cosmos after being buried for an eternity in some black hole in outer space.

Still, she needed to make some attempt at reason before she let herself be consumed by the whirlpool.

She cast him a reproving glance. 'You know, you behaved shockingly in that restaurant.'

'I know.' He looked contrite. 'You're right. I was a disgrace. I should apologise to the restaurant.'

Unconvinced by his humility, she said sternly, 'It was such a *risk*. I can hardly believe it happened.' She shook her head in despair. 'You've done some reckless things, Sandro, but that's the most wicked I ever remember you being.'

His edged his brows pensively together, then he met her

gaze, a gleam in his dark eyes. 'No, *tesoro*. No, I would say that I can be more wicked than that.'

She gasped, scandalised. 'In a *restaurant*?'

He shrugged. 'Anywhere, truthfully. A restaurant, a church. If I have Lara Meadows beside me, there are no limits to the wickedness I can be inspired to.'

'Oh, *you*.' She gave his arm a punch, and after a moment of walking in a silence that clamoured with Alessandro's unspoken laughter she bit her lip and tried again. 'You know, I did say this wouldn't be a date.' Even to her own ears her protest sounded feeble.

He smiled. 'You did, I know.'

'So—so why did you—you know, kiss me like that? And then there was last night… That was just an *outrage*. If the P&C committee ever found out what I'd done in that schoolyard…'

'What's the P&C Committee?'

'Parents and interested Citizens. If they had any idea…' She shuddered, picturing the public outcry.

He slowed to a halt under a street lamp, and took her other hand as well. 'You know why I do these things. I am a man. What else am I to do? You're so beautiful, your lips are so luscious…' His voice thickened. 'And you belong to me…'

'Oh. Oh, well…' She was stirred to her bone marrow, and her voice went all wobbly and husky. 'You know what Holly Golightly said. People can't belong to people. And it's—no excuse. You can't just kiss everyone you like the look of. I told you this would be a meeting.'

'A lovers' meeting.' His warm, sure grip firmed on her hands and she felt pleasure flow in her veins like wine. 'We're lovers, aren't we?'

'Were. We *were* lovers.'

'We will always be lovers, Larissa.' He said it with such seriousness, she had to believe he meant it. He took her shoulders. 'And I don't want to kiss everyone I like the look of.' Whether it was the effect of the wine, or the after-effects of the restaurant, his voice deepened with a sincerity she couldn't deny, and his eyes glowed with an ardent light. 'Only you. Always, always, I want to kiss you.'

Her heart seized, then lurched into a rapid, bumpy rhythm.

She gripped his arms. 'Oh, Alessandro,' she said, breathless and trembling with emotion, 'I wish—I wish I could believe that.'

'Believe it,' he said firmly, pulling her close and kissing her with a conviction that set her veins ablaze and made her erotic regions tingle with longing.

'Hurry,' he said, desire in his eyes, urgency in his voice. 'Let's walk fast.'

The last remaining blocks were like a dream of life the way it could have been, floating along the pavements of old Sydney, hand in hand with her lover, reckless and wild, hunger in her veins.

He ushered her through the Seasons entrance and across the lobby. At the lifts, she flashed him a smile and murmured, 'Déjà-vu.'

The ride up to the thirtieth floor was silent, the air drumming with desire, her thudding heartbeat, and magic visions of the past. She might have been racked with desire, but odd thoughts still crept up on her as he stood beside her in the pulsing silence. One of them being if she'd known this was going to happen, she'd have put in some serious work at a gym.

And another one. What about when he saw her scar? How would he react? And then there were the traces left by her pregnancy and a year of breastfeeding. Her nipples weren't exactly the same sweet pink raspberries he'd adored.

For God's sake, would she remember *what to do*?

Alessandro unlocked his door and stood aside for her. At once the room's atmosphere rushed to meet her.

Ah. The suite.

CHAPTER ELEVEN

IT WASN'T exactly the same, of course. Lara supposed it must have been refurbished over the years, because once she was through the foyer, she saw that the colours seemed different in the glow of the lamps, warmer and more vibrant. In fact, the windows were not in the position she remembered either, so perhaps it wasn't the same suite. But the *feeling* was the same.

And the bed. That low, wide, sleek bed. The covers had been turned down, the pillows fluffed up. So enticing. So—sexual.

Her heart pounded with a nervy, excited rhythm.

Alessandro slipped off his jacket, sending her an assessing glance. 'Would you like anything? Some wine?'

Lara shook her head. 'No. No, thanks. Could we dim the lights a bit, do you think?'

His brows twitched but he barely hesitated. 'Of course.'

In fact the room was already quite softly lit, but he switched off all the lamps, except for one by the bed. Then he dragged the counterpane from the bed and tossed it onto a chair, strolled across and parted the curtains a little, then walked back to her, pulling off his tie and loosening his collar.

Her pulse thundered in her ears. He stood before her, so straight and tall and darkly gorgeous, his eyes all at once so serious and compelling, the shadows in her heart were swamped by emotion. She could feel the electric tension in him, the fierce current that connected him to her at a deep, primitive level.

It all felt so familiar. How many times had she been at this point with him before? And apart from that first unforgettable time, what had followed from this moment had always flowed as naturally and as free of inhibition as the rhythm of life. But it had all been less complicated then. Though tonight… Undeniably, the same dark, smouldering current was there, pulling her to him as powerfully as the sun.

His dark eyes glowed beneath lids that were heavy and slumberous. He slid his thumb across her cheekbone as if she were some exotic beauty. 'I have longed to be with you again.'

He spoke with such intensity, the words wrapped in his beautiful, deep accent, she felt her insides curl up as though licked by fire.

'Have you?' she breathed. 'Me too.' Her voice sounded husky with the intense emotion overflowing in her heart. 'I've never, never stopped thinking of you.'

He reached for the top button on her coat, his quick supple fingers sliding from one to the next, and she felt cooler air flood in as the coat fell to the floor.

How crazy she'd been, how ridiculous to have felt nervous. Once she was trapped in his scorching hot gaze, the desire already smouldering in her blood blew through her like a desert wind, and another Lara, the wild, primitive Lara, took over.

The moment their lips touched, the fire in her sprang to blazing life. His kiss was hot and sexual, and she responded with all she had, aroused by the sensual delights of lip and tongue in sexy collision, relishing his urgent hands curving around her breasts, moulding the undulations of waist and hip, caressing her inflamed nipples.

Starved of sensation for so long, her skin burned for contact. She pressed herself to his hard angular frame, purring at the graze of his long, muscled thighs against hers, while the secret tissues between her legs flamed. Her greedy hands became possessed of their own convulsive life, lusting to enjoy him to the max, to clutch at his black silky hair, smooth the nape of his strong neck, knead his powerful shoulders.

As one kiss dissolved to the next, each deeper and more searching than the last, everything about him—his feel and taste, his strong, sure touch—all felt so achingly familiar, so beloved, and so much *hers*.

In the past he'd been gentle and considerate, his fierce male dominance tempered by tenderness. Tonight, though gentle enough, he was uncompromising, hard and firm and confident, and there was no holding back her instinctive response. With every part of her so hot and aroused, an explosive cocktail of excitement and emotion coursing through her veins, this could be no polite engagement. The heavy beat of passion seethed in her blood and flamed for immediate assuagement.

As though in tune with her urgency Alessandro broke the kiss to trail hot, searing kisses down her neck, slipping his hand under her hair to seek the zip on her dress. She raised her hands in an attempt to take charge of that herself, but he caught them and held them still.

'I'll do this,' he bit out, his deep voice a husky growl.

Then he tugged down the zip and ruthlessly pulled the dress to her waist himself, the flame in his eyes flaring as her breasts were revealed, swelling from the lacy black bra.

He bent his head to scorch them with his lips, the faint roughness of his jaw on her tender skin sending wild quivers of pleasure radiating through her heated flesh.

'Oh,' she gasped, her knees liquefying. 'Oh.'

Then through the black lace of her bra, his mouth closed over one of her nipples. With a provocative playfulness he teased each aching peak, until her lust roared through her like a forest blaze and she yearned for her skin to be exposed.

'Quickly,' she gasped.

Unable to wait for the niceties of gently escalating foreplay, she felt galvanised by a breathless haste to be naked. She dragged down her dress and stepped out of it, unfastened her bra and whipped down her pants, kicking them aside to stand there nude except for her stay-up stockings.

With a wild animal growl Alessandro seized her breasts in his hands and bent his head to kiss them. She moaned, then, as if riding the same desperate whirlwind as she, he dragged his shirt loose and began tearing at the buttons, his lustful gaze mesmerised by the silky blonde triangle at the juncture of her thighs. She tried to help him, her clumsy fingers colliding with his in their haste.

His shirt fell open, revealing his wide, bronzed chest, adorned by sexy whorls of black hair that arrowed down beneath his belt.

For an instant, she paused, the heavy erotic beat in her blood tinged with emotion at the sight of his raw, remembered beauty. Then with a small involuntary cry she bent to kiss his olive satin skin, as scorchingly hot as her own.

With an insatiable thirst to reclaim what was hers, she caressed the strongly defined muscles of his chest with sensual hands and lips, traced the ridges of his ribs, relished the hard-packed muscle of his abdomen.

She reached for his belt buckle at the same time as he, her urgency intermingled with responding to his wild kisses and increasingly fierce caresses, until their frenzied hands released the fastenings and he dragged off the rest of his clothes.

He stood before her, naked, and she felt an involuntary moistening between her thighs as the majestic length and thickness of his proud erection set her juices flowing in tingling expectation. But hardly giving her a moment to take in the full impact of his sleek, raw beauty, the power and heart-stopping grace of his long limbs, Alessandro pushed her onto the bed and threw himself down beside her.

She lay there, burning for the relief of his lean angular body in friction with hers, to feel his body hair brushing her breasts and legs, but first he leaned up on his elbow and reached for a package on the bedside table.

She sat up, and with avid, trembling hands helped him to

slide on the protective sheath, with a fervent mental prayer that *this* one she could trust.

'I've dreamed of you,' he said, gazing down at her nudity, dark eyes ablaze, his voice hoarse and rough with passion. 'Like this. Hot and wild.'

The breath caught in her lungs.

She gazed up into his fierce, passionate face, her heart nearly spilling over with the most intense and poignant love and her need to express it, but she held herself back from framing the words, and reached up to kiss him instead.

He kissed her down onto the pillow, then parted her thighs, his smouldering gaze on her patch of blonde curls, and moved over her, supporting himself on his powerful arms.

She lay trembling beneath him in anticipation, ablaze to the feel of his masculine hair grazing her breasts and legs, tingling to feel the thrust of his hard length filling her.

'Wrap your legs around me,' he commanded, a flame in his black eyes.

Complying, she felt his hard rod tantalise the yearning portals of her moist sex, and melted to the hot, liquid rush deep in her womb. Then, watching her face with his aroused, heavy-lidded gaze, he plunged into her, his eyes closing an instant as if to savour the exquisite pleasure as he filled her with his hot, hard flesh.

Then he rocked her, slowly, gently at first, then harder, faster, with deep, sensual thrusts that made her breath come in gasping little cries. And, oh, the pleasure. She thrilled to the sexy rhythm, her passion fuelled by his athletic stroking of the sensitive, inflamed walls inside her. His rock-hard shaft glided deeper and deeper, faster and harder, in an escalating jungle beat of pure, primitive masculine possession.

Almost at once her excitement made the dizzy, steep reckless climb to the heights of ecstasy, and exploded in a blissful release of spasmodic waves that radiated pleasure throughout her entire body.

Alessandro reached his own climax shortly after, then withdrew from her body, and rolled back onto the pillows. After a few silent, heart-thundering minutes, he stood up and walked into the bathroom. She heard the rush of water, taps flowing, then he returned, glancing down at her with his warm shimmering gaze before joining her and lying on his back, his eyes closed.

Lara lay there as her tumultuous heart rate calmed, in the sweet, exhausted limbo between rapture and afterglow. After a moment Alessandro turned on his side, and leaned up on one elbow to gaze down at her, tracing the line of her body with one finger. 'That's one of the things I've always loved about you. Your ability to respond to the moment.'

Smiling, she turned to her lover, just reaching up to caress his lean, shadow-rough jaw, when her gaze was trapped by the flash of the digital display of a clock radio on the bedside table.

10:40. Arghhh. Her brain snapped out of its pleasant miasma.

'Oh,' she gasped. 'Oh, my God, look at the time. I'm late. I'll be late.'

She leaped from the bed, scrabbled on the floor for her pants and pulled them on, then threw on her dress, diving for her coat before she'd even done up the zip. She pounced on her bra, waved it helplessly for a second, then shrugged the coat on, stuffing the bra into a pocket while she searched for her shoes.

A deep growl intruded on her exertions. Alessandro was sitting up in the bed, his lean, austere face a mask of incredulity.

'I told you, I have to go. I can't stay, sorry.' She cast about for her purse.

'*Per carità.* You can't go *now.* What about...?' His voice was a deep howl of outrage. 'We have hardly begun. That was too—too *fast.* We need now to take it slowly. To let the passion build. To prolong our pleasure until we are both at the—'

'I know. But that's all I have time for. Honestly.' She seized on her purse and turned for the door. 'Thank you, darling,' she said softly, blowing him a kiss. 'It was...splendid.'

'Now, stop right there.' He sprang off the bed, and strode towards her, his tall, bronzed, hair-roughened body still glistening with a faint sheen of sweat after their athletic coupling. Truly, it tore her heart to leave him. 'What can possibly be more urgent?'

She evaded his outstretched hands and backed away. 'Mum's waiting for me. I told you. I can't let her down. I must get home for Vivi.'

He closed his eyes and winced. 'Oh, yes, yes, of course. I'll drive you,' he asserted, swooping on his underwear.

'There isn't time,' she said hurriedly, dashing for the door before he could touch her, her words falling over each other in her haste. 'Honestly. I'll catch a taxi downstairs. Bye.'

The door closed behind her. Cursing with artistic versatility, Alessandro dragged on his trousers, snatched a sweater from a drawer, and, still stumbling into his shoes, hopped to the phone and dialled the concierge.

Three interminable lift minutes later, he sprinted across the lobby and caught her standing outside the entrance, just as his hired BMW swept into the driveway.

'No need to worry, *tesoro*,' he said, smoothly taking her arm and hustling her to the car. 'I'm here now.'

CHAPTER TWELVE

'THANKS for a fabulous time.' Lara leaned across and kissed Alessandro's lips. She noticed him unfastening his seat belt. 'No need to get out.' She reached for the door handle. 'I'll just dash. Do I look all right?'

She glanced down at herself to ensure she was decent, and lifted her bag, gathering herself for the leap out into the cold night air.

Alessandro placed his hand on her thigh. 'I want to see her.'

Her limbs froze. After a stunned second she turned to stare at him and forced herself to reply normally. 'Oh. Are you sure?'

He inclined his head slightly, his dark eyes cool and level. 'I am sure. I'll come in with you.'

'Oh.' An unreasoning terror gripped her. 'She'll be asleep.'

Without replying he got out of the car, and she had no option but to do the same. Walking up to the porch with him in a sort of numb trance, she thought helplessly of how it had been this time last night. Last night he'd been content never to see Vivi or know a personal thing about her. Support from afar, wasn't that the agreed position?

She had the giddy sensation that all her worst nightmares were about to be realised. Once he saw her…

Her heart plunged. How would he *not* want her?

She inserted her key into the lock, then at the last instant turned and faced him, her back to the door. Her throat felt drier than the Gibson Desert. 'Are you sure this is what you want? Didn't you say you'd be better off not knowing anything about her?'

His eyes shimmered with comprehension and she felt so ashamed to be revealing her fear, but there was no containing it.

'She is already alive in my mind,' he said quietly. 'How can I not see her?'

Somehow her hand turned the key, and she opened the door.

Alessandro stepped into a foyer. It was lit by a lamp and smelled like lemon furniture polish. Inside the door was a hallstand with a mirror, various coats and hats hanging from its hooks. What struck him about it immediately and sent a pang searing through him was a small yellow raincoat.

Lara led him past a set of French doors to a flight of stairs at the rear. He noticed childish paintings pinned to the wall, then his eye followed them all the way up the staircase.

He placed his foot on the lowest stair, conscious of a sudden rise in his blood pressure. He mounted the stairs behind Lara, his anticipation increasing with every step. By the time he reached the landing on the upper floor, his heart had quickened to a ridiculous gallop.

Curiosity. It was only natural.

He stood back while Lara paused outside a white-painted door and gave a soft special knock, then followed her inside.

He was in an airy, comfortably furnished sitting room, divided by an archway from a small dining room and kitchen. French doors led to the narrow balcony he'd seen from the street, but they were closed now. The room was pleasantly warm, courtesy of a fireplace with low flames leaping behind glass.

There were books, pot-plants and flowers, pictures on the walls, but he couldn't take it all in, focused as he was on one thing only.

'Mum, I've brought Alessandro.'

He glanced around and saw Lara's mother rise from the

sofa where she'd obviously been reading in the light of a standard lamp. At Lara's words she exchanged a glance with her daughter, then turned her warm gaze on him.

Her shrewd blue eyes examined what felt like every atom of his soul, then she held out her hand and clasped his warmly. 'Good to see you, Alessandro.' She glanced back at Lara. 'I'll leave you to it, dear.' She kissed Lara's cheek. 'See you in the morning.'

Lara murmured something to her mother, then the older woman gathered her things and left, closing the door behind her.

Once he and Lara were alone, tension crackled in the room higher than the flames in the fireplace. She looked white, her face set as if for an ordeal, her eyes strained and shadowy.

'Will you wait here a second?' She gestured to him to stand still and not move, then left to hurry through a door leading from the dining room. She came back a few moments later, still pale, but looking resigned.

'All right.' She sent him an appeal in her glance. 'You'll—you'll have to promise not to wake her.'

He could hear her anxiety, but what reassurance could he offer? It was his right to see his child, and he was claiming it. He merely nodded and followed when she motioned him.

With the blood suddenly pounding in his ears he was hardly aware of the room she showed him to, just a blurred impression of deep rose and white surroundings, the narrow bed with a net canopy like the bower of a fairy-tale princess, and the little girl.

At first sight of her his heart seized. She was sleeping on her side, her cheek on the pillow, so he couldn't at once see her face in total.

A toadstool lamp by the bed shed a soft light on her head of silky dark hair. Her rosy lips were parted, and incredibly long, curly dark lashes fanned in a perfect semi-circle against the softest, purest cheek he'd ever laid eyes on.

The breath constricted in his lungs. As he stared, immobilised, drinking in her exquisiteness, her long lashes gave a few rapid tremors and she made a restless movement and flung out one arm.

'She's dreaming,' Lara whispered, bending to gently rescue a worn-looking doll in danger of being crushed. She replaced the covers over the girl's small shoulders.

After a few thundering minutes, or it might have been hours, Lara telegraphed a querying look at him and he roused himself from his trance to gaze at her across the divide. She dropped her eyes, defensive and inaccessible, even though the naked imprint of her slim, nubile body was so freshly seared into his own.

He returned with her to the sitting room, but didn't stay to talk. With the uproar pounding in his head and the storm in his soul he needed to be alone.

The last thing he remembered was Lara standing on the staircase, watching him leave, her hands contorting before her.

CHAPTER THIRTEEN

LARA woke late, with an immediate sense of something irrevocable having happened. Even the sensual impression left by Alessandro's lips and hands and big lean frame was overwhelmed by her anxiety. Her restless night had taken its toll.

She lingered in her bed, torn by conflicting fears.

If only she had some way of predicting what he might do. Now that he'd seen Vivi, would his curiosity be satisfied? Would he go on his way and never look back at his child? At her?

She felt a deep wrench within her. True, that had been what she'd *thought* she wanted, but now…

With a rush of certainty she knew it would *not* be for the best. Not for Vivi.

As for herself… He'd said some wonderful things to her last night, things she could have sworn were sincere, but so he had the last time he was here. She'd put all her faith in them then, and love and trust had turned to bitterness and heartbreak.

Even now, if he said he loved her, if by some wild turn of the card he decided he wanted to marry her, could she crush down her hurt and misgivings over his casual treatment of her in the past and go through with it?

A misty little fantasy nudged its way in through the barriers. The scenario in which seeing Vivi last night had inspired him. He'd been enchanted. He'd understood then how beautiful and special a gift a child was, and he felt proud of her. So proud. He'd decide to stay and be a proper father. He'd marry Lara, not because she was the mother of his child but because he *loved* her, and when they went walking he'd hold Vivi's hand, and Vivi would have a dad she could take to the Year One Father's Day Picnic...

Her throat thickened and tears rushed into her eyes. Even if all that miraculously happened and she hadn't absolutely blown her chances by telling him straight off that she *wouldn't* marry him, could she do it simply because he wanted Vivi? Wouldn't the old betrayal always be there, undermining their happiness?

And how likely was the Marquis of the Venetian Isles to give up his sophisticated globe-trotting lifestyle for domestic bliss?

She cancelled the fantasy, reached for a tissue and gave her eyes a good wipe.

As usual, Vivi was up and about, probably since first light like a little bird. Lara could hear her voice from her playroom, singing to Kylie Minogie one minute, ordering her to sit up straight and pay attention or march to the time-out room the next.

She roused herself and drifted in to greet her darling, then wandered into her bathroom.

There was so much to consider, she mused, surrendering her nakedness to the soothing stream. So what if he'd had his marriage annulled? Did she seriously think he might *not* have had other girlfriends since that time? Did she care about all of them?

Of course she didn't. She only cared about the Giulia affair.

Bathed, semi-dressed and wrapped in her towelling robe, she ironed her blouse, then Vivi's school dress, while Vivi gouged a hole in the Vegemite with a knife and inexpertly smeared the massive lump on her toast. Lara paused to watch her take a bite, and winced in sympathy when her little elfin face screwed up in horror. Ugh.

At work Lara was faced with a heavier than usual pile of manuscripts submitted by aspiring authors. She grimaced. Fantastic.

Her worries kept intruding. Despite her feelings about Alessandro's marriage to that woman, could she seriously contemplate just letting him walk away? She knew she wasn't up to another airport scene. The last one had nearly killed her, and then she'd been sure he was coming *back*.

She forced herself back to the manuscript she was reading, and realised she was on page two without having taken in a word. Something about a possum and a tree house. Hopeless, she realised, and airlifted it to the waste basket.

But how could she stop him? Other women seemed able to dig their claws in and hold onto men. Her lack of ability to do so had already been clearly demonstrated to the world.

She opened another masterpiece, her heart sinking in misgiving when she thought of his face when he'd left last night. He'd looked so stern and remote, so closed off from her. If only she could get some inkling of how he was feeling today. She really needed to *see* him. Find out how he looked.

It was agony, knowing he was just a short walk away down the corridor, yet out of her reach. She supposed she could hardly mosey along and interrupt the interviews going on in there for the new MD's position. Not to mention that Donatuila was forever present, guarding him like a mastiff.

She drummed her fingers on the pages spread before her on the desk. Soon he would be leaving.

Panic seized her. Her time was running out. Once he got on that plane it would be the end of everything. Her absolute *joy*. The excitement of not knowing what he would do next, the sheer thrill of being with him, the passion. He'd fly out of their lives and she'd be back to her nun-like existence.

Anguish speared through her at the thought of losing him again. How would she ever bear it?

She turned a page and puzzled over a strange sentence for a while, then gave up and aimed it for the bin. Another slam dunk. Why couldn't people learn to punctuate?

She was reaching for the next one on the pile just as the

phone rang on her desk. She started, and her heart jumped into a nervy racketing.

'Lara?' It was Alessandro's deep voice. 'Can I see you for a few minutes?'

'Certainly,' she said. Calmly, she hoped.

She didn't feel calm. She replaced the phone with shaking hands, realising this was it. The verdict. After a few seconds, avoiding Josh's interested glance, she stood up, straightened her blouse and soft blue jacket, and brushed down her pencil skirt.

Alessandro was waiting for her at the door of his office. She tried to read his expression, but he looked controlled and inscrutable. He closed the door behind her when she walked in, then bent to brush her cheek with lips that were cool.

'Good morning, Lara.'

Lara. Not Larissa, or *carissima*, or *tesoro*. After being lovers last night, they were back to being formal.

Some expensive, tangy aftershave lingered on his lean, smooth-shaven jaw. He looked so tall, dark and delicious in his charcoal suit and crisp blue shirt, on another, less nerve-racking occasion, she might have kissed his beautiful, stern mouth. It was easy to believe he was the Marquis of the Venetian Isles, though impossible to credit that such a gorgeous, sophisticated example of masculinity had ever desired *her*.

Maybe she'd dreamed last night and those things he'd said. Maybe, when he'd left her afterwards with that remote, closed expression, it was because at heart he was repelled by the modest domesticity of her and her child.

She managed to stay upright on her legs, but her entire being was a vessel of nervous flutterings.

'So?' she queried in a low voice, her heart on a cliff's edge, last night's scene with Vivi vivid in her mind. 'What— what is it?'

His brilliant gaze scoured her face in careful assessment, then he lowered his lashes. Choosing his words, she realised, her heart plunging in fear.

'I have been thinking. I want to meet Vivi.'

'Oh.' The shock roiled through her. She felt her heart rev into a painful pounding rhythm. The moisture dried from her throat. 'Oh, good, good,' she somehow said, knowing she had to behave like an adult, her dry voice as husky as a crow's. 'But…are you sure? Where are you going with this, Sandro? Are you aware…? I—I mean, have you considered this will be deeply—*emotional* and significant to her?'

Her voice cracked on 'emotional', and there was no concealing her feelings.

'I am doing what I must do, *carissa*.' He frowned. 'Why are you so afraid? Last night was deeply emotional and significant to *me*. All of it.'

'Oh.' Her eyes filled with tears, and she dashed them away with the backs of her hands. 'All right, then,' she said, when she could. She moistened her lips. 'So what happens after you meet her? You fly off to the other side of the globe and we never see you again?'

'That's not how it will be.'

'How will it be, then?' Her hands twisted in tune with her churning heart. 'Can you see this—that if you meet her, then leave her and never come back, she will be more destroyed by it than if you *never* meet her?'

Shock flickered in his dark eyes, and he grabbed her shoulders. 'Why do you have such a poor opinion of me, Lara? Why would I do that? Do you think I would just forget her?'

'I don't know. You forgot me.'

His eyes widened. *'Cosa?'*

There was a knock. Alessandro released her just as the door opened and Donatuila swished in.

'Your next guy is here, boss.' She came to a surprised halt, her pencilled brows flying up. 'Oh, hey. Sorry. Am I interrupting?'

'Oh, no, no,' Lara said, whipping blindly around and

managing to make the door without knocking her sideways.
'I'm just leaving.'

She walked briskly to the ladies' room, grateful not to
meet any other curious eyes along the way, and sat in a
cubicle until the tears had properly dried up and she'd
stopped the shaking.

How ironic, to have been interrupted in the middle of what
might have been the most important conversation of her life.

After a while, she got up and checked her mascara, though
there wasn't much she could do without make-up. She'd just
have to wait for her eyes to return to normal. Why was it that
some tears did more damage than others?

Back at her desk, she reached for the next manuscript on
the pile and kept her eyes lowered to it. There may have been
a charged silence in the room, but if any of her friends noticed
anything, they didn't say a word.

It was nearly lunch time when an eruption in the depths of
her bag summoned her to her mobile. Her mother, she
assumed. Something to do with picking Vivi up from school.

Her heart jolted when she saw that the message was from
Alessandro.

Meet me in the lobby.

Fine, she thought, straightening her spine. Round two. She
was calmer now. She'd had coffee, she wasn't blotchy any more,
and she'd had time to think a little. If he wanted to see Vivi, that
could only be good, couldn't it? Wasn't it what she wanted?

She dropped by the Ladies first to make sure she looked
smooth and pale, the most she could hope for on this stress-
ful day.

Alessandro was in the lobby ahead of her. She saw him as
soon as the lift doors opened on the ground floor. He was
standing by the entrance, chatting to some guy from Sales.

He turned his dark intelligent gaze to her as she approached, and she saw his lean face tauten, then smooth to
become controlled.

Anxious not to cause any more interest than she was sure had been already aroused, she walked straight past them, through the glass doors and out into the street.

After a few minutes, she heard a firm, energetic tread behind her and Alessandro caught up.

'Are you all right?' He looked searchingly down at her, and she met his gaze coolly enough.

'Fine. I think.'

'I'm sorry about before, *tesoro*. I have been trying all day, but the office is not a good place for conversation. Let's see if we can do better.' He glanced around for a suitable location. At a nearby corner he spotted a leafy little precinct of shops and cafés. Taking her elbow, he hustled her to it, steering her under an awning shared by a café and a florist shop, halting her next to a giant tub of fragrant stocks. Deceived into believing it was spring, masses of freesias, daffodils and jonquils perfumed the heady air.

Alessandro glanced at his watch, his brows edging together. In contrast with the flowers, he smelled fresh and crisp and masculine. 'I've managed to get some tickets for tonight's opera. I thought perhaps you might come with me, enjoy the music, and afterwards we can have a little supper while we make our arrangements?'

'Arrangements?' She glanced warily at him.

His eyes were cool, steady and determined. 'For me to meet with Vivi. I know you must prepare her, but we also need to consider how and where it should happen. Don't we, *carissa*? We want it to be—good.'

Her pulse quickened, but she had more control this time. 'That's a lovely invitation, Alessandro, but I'm afraid I can't accept. I—I can't go out another night and leave Vivi with Mum.' His brows lifted, and she said hurriedly, 'Mum doesn't mind, but it would be the third night in a row I've asked her to babysit. She has to work, and it's very tiring for her. Last night I barely made it home in time for her.' Conscious of the glint in his eyes piercing her right through her cerebral cortex, she added, 'There'd hardly be time for us to talk, anyway. I'd have to come home straight after the opera, and—' She shrugged and lowered her gaze, mumbling, 'And anyway, Vivi needs me to be with her.'

His face became smooth and expressionless, and he nodded his head. 'I see. So many reasons. Well, well, of course she does need you… It's a pity. It does make it quite difficult for me. I don't have very much time before I go to my next appointment in Bangkok.'

He glanced at his watch again, his jaw set grimly, and started to move away, negative vibrations whirling. Then all at once he turned back and gripped her arm, sending a bolt of pleasurable electricity searing through her flesh. 'Is this *reluctance* because you're angry about my marriage to Giulia? Is that why you accused me of forgetting you?'

Perhaps because she'd been so stirred up earlier, her emotions all sprang to the fore, ready for another workout.

She drew herself up to her full five seven. '*What?* I'm not reluctant. That's a ridiculous thing to say. Look, what you don't seem to realise is that when you're a parent you can't just drop everything at a whim. I do want you to know Vivi. I *do*. But I can't help your time frame. If you just appear every six years, hang around for a few days then disappear again— that's not my fault, is it?'

His mouth and jaw tightened. 'That is the work I do. That is how my life is.'

She shrugged. 'Well, there you are. And as for you forgetting me—well, too right you did. What else am I to think? One minute you were here with *me*, then five minutes later you married *her*.'

A flush darkened the bronzed skin of his lean cheek. 'If only I *had* forgotten you.' He breathed so hard his nostrils flared. 'It was you who feared to fly away with me, remember? When I married Giulia I didn't expect you to know or even care. But—' he raised both of his hands in a very Italian gesture '—since you clearly *do* need to know, I'll tell you all of it. I married her because it was necessary for her to have a husband.'

A searing pain stabbed her heart at the same instant as some scalding hot emotion shot straight to her head. 'Why? Was she pregnant too?'

He closed his eyes, his flush deepening, and said through gritted teeth, *'Don't…'* Then he held up a hand, as if to forestall her from repeating the frightful word. 'No, she was not *pregnant.*' His consonants were so closely clipped he almost bit the words out. 'She was afraid.'

Relief made her legs go like jelly, and to her surprise and severe annoyance she backed into the tub of stocks and her knees gave way. Alessandro's hands shot out to grab her, an instant before her bottom hit the water level.

With a shocked, concerned expression, he steadied her and pulled her onto her feet, helped her to brush her flustered self down, and drew her away before she could do any more damage to the merchandise.

The florist emerged from the shop interior. She broke into a beam when Alessandro turned to placate her, his hands flying about in profuse expressions of regret.

The ignominy of falling into a tub and having stalks stick into her didn't soothe Lara's jagged feelings. It hardly helped her swallow pathetic explanations as to why he'd had to marry that woman.

Afraid indeed. She checked the back of her skirt. Afraid of what? Scared D&G might get a divorce?

Part of her was aware of Alessandro apologising about the stocks, insisting on buying them all, writing something on the back of a card for the florist. Lara picked up on him cementing his relationship with the gushing woman by selecting a further bunch of freesias and paying her, seducing her utterly with his potent charm formula.

Typical, Lara glowered. Perhaps the florist was scared of getting her flowers crushed. Perhaps he should marry *her*.

She might have actually muttered some of that aloud, because she felt Alessandro's gaze swivel around to examine her. Judging by the acute glance piercing her skull, he might have caught some of her words.

When the woman had taken the freesias inside to wrap, he said in a low, casual voice, 'As a matter of fact, she was scared of her ex-husband.'

'Yeah, was she?'

He looked intently at her. 'Yes, she was. Gino was a hot-headed guy. He'd abused her. It was one of those—obsessive situations where he couldn't accept the end of their marriage. He continually threatened her. Doesn't this sort of thing happen here? She was terrified.' His dark eyes hardened with recollection. 'She felt she needed to live with someone who could protect her.'

She nodded, just managing not to roll her eyes. 'Oh, the poor little woman. Right. Of course she needed to live with you. What else could she have done? Oh, and she had to *marry* you. Naturally. I see that.'

His eyes lit with an intense piercing gleam, and she found it hard to maintain her cool, breezy façade because inside she was simmering with fury.

Well, well, well. How very convenient to have a handsome *marchese* on hand to marry when the going got rough. Never mind that that *marchese* belonged to another woman on the other side of the world. A woman he'd promised to return to. A woman with genuine *need* of him.

Her words seemed to have piqued more than his curiosity. That gleam in his eyes wasn't too far from satisfaction—possibly even amusement. If he hadn't been looking so tall and lean and intelligent, so edible with his black hair and olive tan in contrast with his Armani suit, blue shirt and purple silk tie, she could have slapped his handsome face.

She restrained herself, only just, but couldn't eliminate a certain tinge of sarcasm from her voice. 'How very noble of you to make such a sacrifice.' She saw his brows lift in aristocratic query, but her indignation spurred her on. 'Why couldn't she have gone to the police, or the courts? They have them in Italy, don't they?'

'Do they always work here in these cases?' he asked mildly.

'Oh…well…' She dismissed that point with a shrug. 'Why couldn't she hire a security firm? Surely she didn't have to marry you.'

'This *was* Italy.' His deep voice was dry and quiet and even. 'And she tried hiring a private firm. The guy bribed her security guard and broke into her flat. He broke all the bones in her face.'

'Oh.' She shuddered in spite of herself. 'That's horrible.'

'Yes, it was.' He grabbed her shoulders, and held her firmly, his gaze suddenly stern. 'And it wasn't *noble* of me. It was no sacrifice. I had nothing to lose, had I, Lara? It was an act of friendship, pure and simple. I have known Giulia since childhood. At one time we were like—brother and sister. She'd tried everything else. She thought that perhaps Gino would finally give up if he believed she belonged to another man.' His hands tightened on her shoulders, then, as though realising that he was manhandling her like the wild beast he truly was, he let go. 'Sorry, sorry,' he said, waving his hands in placatory gestures. 'As it happened—Giulia knew of my— upbringing and my feelings about violence against women, so I guess she thought she could come to me.'

Oh, great. Kicked off the moral high ground by a victim of domestic violence. Shame and embarrassment flooded in to dilute her anger and turn her into a confused mess.

'Oh,' she said brusquely, straightening her jacket. 'Right. Well, then. She was very—fortunate to have you, wasn't she?' She forced a faux gracious smile, and made a stilted effort to recover some ground. 'And I guess, if you were fancy free…if you had no commitments anywhere *else*, why not?'

His eyes glinted. 'What commitments did I *know* that I had, *carissa*? Weren't you the girl who needed time to think?'

She gasped. 'Look, that wasn't a no.'

'In what way wasn't it one?'

'Well, why couldn't you have been more...?' She gave herself a little shake and sighed in exasperation. 'All right, so what happened when you—ended the marriage?'

'Her ex was a racing driver. You might have heard of him. Gino Ricci? No? He died in a crash soon after the wedding.' He shook his head. 'Not so surprising, if you knew him. Our marriage was entirely a sham. It was intended to last just as long as it took Gino to move on. Tragically, he went one step too far. When he killed himself there was no further need for it, so...' He shrugged and opened his hands.

'*Well*, you certainly went to a lot of trouble for a sham. Designer wedding gowns, if I remember correctly, the press invited in, spreads about your *palazzo*. The gold leaf on your ceiling frescoes, your old family retainers... Your town house in London, your view of the Thames, your red Ferrari...'

He looked apologetic. 'You need to understand, Larissa. In many ways it's a different world over there from what you are used to here.'

Flushing, she cast him a glowering glance. 'No doubt. The Meadows family doesn't quite run to *palazzos*, I suppose.'

He made a rueful twitch of his brows, and stared thoughtfully at some passers-by, then flashed her a smile. 'That would have been the old Lamborghini, I think. And there is only one family retainer.' He shoved his hands in his pockets and leaned his big frame against the shop door jamb. 'That gold leaf is flaking, by the way. It needs restoring quite badly.' He flickered a glance over her. 'If you were following it I'm surprised you didn't read about our annulment. It was reported quite widely in the Italian press.'

'Maybe I lost interest,' she said coldly. 'I probably had other things on my mind.'

He winced and turned away, just as the florist returned with the mass of freesias, attractively wrapped now in purple tissue, and counted the change into his hand with adoring eyes. Anyone would have thought the silly woman was in *love* with him.

He accepted the bunch, then with a small ironic flourish passed it to Lara.

'Oh,' she said, taken aback. 'Well. Well, thank you.'

The florist tore herself away to retreat into the shop, and Lara said in a gruff, constrained voice, 'You—mentioned your—your upbringing. What did you mean? Are you saying there was domestic violence?'

'You could say so.'

Mortified, she said stiffly, 'I'm sorry, I didn't mean to sound—dismissive.'

His dark eyes gleamed. 'Dismissive? No, I'm not sure dismissive is quite the word, *carissa*.'

She raised her brows coolly, though her voice sounded as rocky as sections of the Bindinong Bypass. 'No? What then, in your opinion?'

He glanced at her, a faint curl to one corner of his mouth, then looked at his watch. 'Talk as we walk. I have someone waiting to be interviewed.'

She strode silently beside him, clutching the flowers, waiting for the verdict though she knew it would be scathing, at a loss to understand how she had managed to land herself in the wrong, when *she* was the one left holding the baby.

How could she have lost all control? Still, she seethed to know what he'd been going to say, however unflattering it might be. She glanced at him a couple of times, but his expression had grown pensive, his sexy mouth set firm.

Was he planning to answer her? Did he want her to *beg*?

He remained silent all the way to the Stiletto building, while her curiosity to know what he'd hinted built to bursting point. At one time she was completely disconcerted when she noticed him shoot her a narrow, thoughtful glance. Just what did *that* mean?

Inside the glass entrance doors, her shaky patience snapped. 'All right, then. Let me have it. *How* did I sound?'

The gleam was back in his eyes. 'Jealous,' he said instantly. 'Like a jealous, spoilt little girl.'

'Oh!' A red hot tidal wave swept from her toes to the top of her head. 'All right, *yes*,' she hissed, 'I was jealous. But let me tell you something, *signor*. That was no little girl's jealousy. That was *big* girl's, *big* time. And if you think I blamed Giulia, you're wrong. I blamed *you*.' She jabbed the freesias at his chest. 'You promised to come back, and, yes, I was waiting for you.' Tears filled her eyes. 'Like a stupid, dumb idiot I believed in you. I *trusted* you.'

Danger flashed from his dark eyes. 'That is a lie. You were *not* at the Centrepoint Tower. I waited there for you for three solid days. I combed this town for you. I phoned and phoned. No reply. I went to your flat... *Nothing.* Other people were living there. Some guy who told me you'd moved to Queensland with your boyfriend. Your *boyfriend*, Lara.'

She gasped as the world whirled around and around her in a crazy kaleidoscope. 'What?' she said faintly, crushing the flowers in her grasp. 'Are you saying...? You came back from America?'

The lift pinged. A crowd of businessmen piled out, and Alessandro waited coolly, then strode in to occupy the vacant lift. He leaned forward to press the button, his glance flicking outside to where she was still standing in a state of stunned bemusement. The doors started their slide.

'Yes,' he said quietly. 'I came back for you. And *you weren't there.*'

He said those last words so accusingly, at the last moment she sprang forward in sudden urgency and wailed, 'But, Sandro. Sandro, don't you understand?'

The doors closed.

CHAPTER FOURTEEN

ALESSANDRO strode from the lift, giving way to a need to loosen his collar after feeling such unaccustomed heat. In an attempt to retrieve his habitual tranquillity, he tried to rationalise the events of the last few days by explaining them to himself in the cool, rational language only a man could understand.

So. A man meets a woman who tells him she has his child. The man wants to help the woman… No. The man is eager to *know* and help the woman *and* the child.

He offers the woman—against his better judgement after what happened the last time—but in total honesty and sincerity—his passion, his affection, but the woman has fears, despite her obvious passion for *him*. Irrational, certainly, but fears nonetheless—that the man will in some way harm the child.

Alessandro felt his blood pressure jump a notch.

The man *sees* his child… At the memory the breath caught in his throat, and he had to stand still as he did every time he thought of those heart-stopping moments. That small, exquisite girl. Her fingertips. That pure, soft skin.

He *sees* her, but knows very well, all the signs are there, that *he*, the father of the child, is excluded from that female circle. An invisible barrier has been erected around the woman and the child. And what for? Is it to do with the past? A past he is in *no way* responsible for?

Alessandro gritted his teeth.

Dio mio, he will smash that barrier with his bare hands if it kills him.

He walked into his office and met Tuila's assessing gaze over the tops of her glasses. He scowled. What was that narrow-eyed look about?

'Did you want to run through the people we've seen so far?' Tuila said.

'What people?'

Tuila's brows shot up. 'Are you kidding?'

He shrugged and kicked out his chair, though he didn't sit down. 'Sure, sure. Whatever.'

She started on the list of interviewees while he paced, hands shoved into his pockets. He would have to be firm. If Lara wouldn't lower her guard he might have to show her the steel edge of his resolve.

'Strike him,' he commanded, raising an imperious hand when Tuila broached the first candidate. She arched her brows, and started in on the next one. 'No, no, forget her,' he ordered. 'Dizzy.'

Lara's behaviour was mystifying. He could see well enough why she'd be upset if she was pregnant and saw that he'd married someone else. But now, everything was different. Here he was, back in the country, quite prepared to…

'Dexter Barry?' Tuila enquired.

'*Per carità*. Are you mad? The man was hopeless.'

'How about Steve Disney? I rather liked him. He was young, bright, well qualified.'

He gave Tuila a long, steel glance. With a shrug she lowered her eyes.

He dragged a hand through his hair. Tonight could have been so fine. The music, the arrangements… He'd actually been looking forward to the planning.

Like—a couple of parents. Then afterwards, he'd have taken her to the hotel, and shown her how fantastic, how joyful it could be.

Sacramento, if he had time, if it were up to him he would show them the world, shower them with *palazzoes* lined with *frescoes* and gold leaf, scatter rose petals at their feet.

He realised with a cold chill that time was running out. In a few days he'd have settled on the managing director, and he'd be boarding that plane for Bangkok without having made Lara understand the first thing about him.

She still had no idea.

Although last night… Hadn't there been that moment in the light of the street lamp when her eyes had been filled with emotion..? And then again afterwards, during the love…?

He closed his eyes while the vision of her loveliness, nude apart from those black stockings, swam before his eyes. *Dio*, the love.

Or had she just given him a little taste of herself to taunt him? The turmoil in his chest deepened. If he hadn't been an optimist, he'd be starting to think they were doomed to end up like the last time. Just like the last time.

He had a grim feeling that he'd be forced to leave soon with everything unresolved with Lara, and without knowing Vivi.

His chest panged. His one child in the world.

And…

He realised in a sudden galvanising panic that if he didn't take matters in hand, in no time Lara would be working for some other guy, who'd inevitably fall in love with her. He could picture it now. Some big, sunburnt, cricket-crazed Australian who'd be spending every minute of every working day plotting to seduce her. Next thing she knew she'd be marrying the guy, while his *daughter*, his little girl…

'What about Roger Hayward? He wasn't so bad, was he? Strong, clever, proactive…'

He started from his meditations. 'Tuila,' he snarled. 'Get a grip.' He slammed his fist on the desk and Tuila jumped. 'None of those clowns will do. Not one of them.'

CHAPTER FIFTEEN

LARA let herself in the gate, still in a stunned haze. All the way home on the train, all she'd been able to think of was Alessandro at the Centrepoint Tower, waiting into the night for the woman who never arrived.

How he must have suffered. His hurt, the disappointment. And, oh, what a bitter assault to his pride. She shied away from imagining his emotions on that return flight without her. *Any* man would have been seething with fury. No wonder he'd been so hostile on his first day at Stiletto.

The amazing thing was that he was still so—giving. He must have really wanted her then. While now… She had a panicked sense that today she'd used up her last chance with him. Somehow she had to find a way to explain at once.

After the flower-shop fiasco she'd found it impossible to see him again before she left work to straighten the record. He'd been ensconced with Tuila all afternoon, and then he must have slipped out while she was lingering at her desk for an opportunity to see him. If Vivi and Greta hadn't been waiting for her she'd have gone to the Seasons after him.

Funny thing was that, now she was allowing herself to dream of it, she could see how wonderful a father he would be. If only there were some way she could stop him from getting on that plane to Bangkok.

Oh, face it, face it, Lara. In deep, all over again. In love with him as hopelessly and passionately as ever. Only now her needs weren't just *her* needs. They were Vivi's as well, and more urgent than ever before.

As usual, at home her mother's eagle eye didn't miss a thing.

'How'd it go?' Greta asked, the minute the hugs and kisses were over and Vivi had made her report on the Year One sandwich selection and the lunchtime tussle in the sandpit. 'Any progress?'

Lara knew exactly what she was referring to. She wanted to know Alessandro's reaction to seeing Vivi. She framed her reply carefully, conscious of small ears having major flapping ability.

'A little.' She met Greta's eyes. 'He wants to—further the acquaintance. He wanted me to meet him tonight to discuss it, only—I didn't think it would be fair to—everyone.' She glanced significantly at Vivi.

A thoughtful look came over Greta's face. 'What if I see if I can swap shifts?' Her eyes glistened. 'Oh, and did I mention? See what came for you.' She pointed Lara up the stairs to her flat, and Lara climbed the stairs, Vivi bounding up ahead of her, Greta bringing up the rear.

She opened her front door and spring burst upon her. Flowers. Dozens of stocks, looking as perky as ever and done up in several heavenly arrangements, along with masses of jonquils, daffies, more of the delicious freesias, purple lisiandras, and roses, roses, roses. The florist must have been cleaned out.

The flat was as fragrant as a hothouse.

'Oh,' Lara gasped. 'Oh.'

She needed no reminding of her ungracious behaviour at the florist's, but in spite of that her heart bounded up in hopeful joy. It was probably natural Alessandro would have had some of them sent to her, since she was the one who'd sat in them— but there was no way she'd sat in *all* of them. Not the lizzies. And she'd certainly have remembered sitting in roses.

How could he have wanted to do something so wonderful, so romantic, after those things she'd snarled at him in the lobby?

Vivi whirled from bunch to bunch, rapturously cooing. 'It's Christmas. It's Christmas.' She turned and looked eagerly up at Lara. 'Is it Christmas, Mummy? Did Santa bring them?'

Lara gazed at her, hesitating. This was a moment in time, she realised. A pivotal moment in Vivi's life. 'Ah. No, well…actually…' She took Vivi's hands. 'Come and sit down over here, my darling, and I'll tell you who sent them.'

A little later, Lara sat on her bed and flipped open her mobile, her urgency to talk to Alessandro sooner rather than later overwhelming all other considerations. Those flowers had to mean something. The outcome could be fantastic, or it could be a disaster. But what was she? A craven coward, or a strong, warm mother with her child's interests at heart?

With her breath on hold, she dialled. Immediately, the number switched to the message service.

All right. Alessandro could be anywhere. She sprang up and paced. He might, or might not, keep to his plan of attending the opera. If she couldn't find him there, she'd visit him at the hotel. Sure, it would be a gamble, but if she did *nothing* she'd never sleep.

It was definitely a moment to be seized. She checked the phone directory, and dialled the Opera House's enquiry number.

Vivi was asleep long before Lara climbed into the taxi, the skirt of her red chiffony dress flaring from the big, warm, black pashmina she'd wrapped around herself. If Greta had been curious as to where she was headed, she kept it to herself, restricting herself to some warmly approving comments about Lara's appearance.

Lara felt a nervy, optimistic excitement. The danger of the operation had ignited a turbulence in her blood like hot, seething lemonade. The last glimpse she'd had of herself in the dressing-table mirror had shown a reckless sparkle in her eyes that she had to admit was really rather flattering.

The taxi cruised through the night into the city, swept down the boulevard of Macquarie Street and circled the roundabout at the Opera House forecourt. She leaned forward, nervously scanning the trickle of people who'd already started to issue from the exits. Limos were queuing at the pick-up bay, but she doubted if Alessandro would have any use for a car.

She paid off the driver, stood getting her bearings for a second, then climbed a little way up the broad sweep of stairs to the platform on which the giant shells of the building rested. While she couldn't cover all the exits, she felt certain Alessandro would choose to walk back to his hotel, and would be bound to pass close enough to this spot for her to see him.

She tried to damp down her nerves. It was important she remain poised and calm. Confident, assured. A woman to be reckoned with. A mother. The mother of his child.

The trickle swelled to a stream, and soon the concourse was a throng of opera patrons, scurrying to snatch taxis, or strolling off in groups and couples towards elegant suppers on Circular Quay. She cast about, hugging her pashmina to her, straining for a sight of one tall man among the many.

Alessandro avoided getting caught up in the crowd at the hat-check, and strolled out onto the concourse, the rich Puccini melodies singing in his blood. And they weren't all that stirred his blood. The sky was clear and cold, the night still young, and desire stalked his veins like a leopard.

The way he remembered it, six years ago Lara had been as passionate and enthusiastic about the evenings they'd shared at the opera as he himself. She'd been so eager to learn. She'd soaked up the music, adored all the stories he raked up from his memory to tell her about the opera legends—the divas, the conductors.

She'd have loved it tonight, he felt sure. And he'd have enjoyed it a thousand times more experiencing the spectacle and the drama through her fresh, bright eyes.

He shook his head, and realised with a heavy ache in his chest that his opportunities were diminishing.

He turned towards the Quay and the stroll to his hotel, resisting the glimpse of the future that of late had kept opening before him with a grim, unwelcome persistence. More cities, more hotels. More solitary evenings. More hollow friendships, made in transit. Empty, meaningless career triumphs. Offices that were other people's workplaces. Nowhere of his own. No life to cling to.

Next thing he knew, he'd be an old man retreating to Venice to live in a mouldering ruin with his mother. What he needed... What he longed for...

'Alessandro. Sandro?'

His heart, his feet, rocked to a sudden halt and he stood stock still, then turned his gaze upwards and to his right. Unless he was hallucinating, Lara was standing right there, on the Opera House steps. Her smile was a little uncertain, but her gaze didn't waver. He watched her take a step down, then another, and he felt joy burst in his heart like a blaze.

'Oh, hi,' she said, an audible breathlessness in her voice. 'I was just passing. I wasn't sure if you'd really be here, but I thought—if you were, maybe you wouldn't mind some company for the little supper?'

'The little supper,' he repeated hazily, his head reeling at how beautiful she looked, wrapped in some black lustrous wool thing that framed her face's delicacy, while some gorgeous flash of red peeped out at her breast and swirled around her knees.

She was all lit up—eyes, lips, her glossy hair—as if by some internal flame.

Anxiety flickered in her eyes. 'That's if—that's if you are still planning to have the little supper.'

His wandering brain made a snap recovery. 'Oh, sure. Sure I am. The supper, of course.' He smiled. 'Lucky for me this was the moment you happened to pass by.'

'It must be Fate,' she said with a gurgle of a laugh that rippled through him.

She stepped down to his level. He was almost unbearably tempted to take her in his arms, hold her vibrant body to him, smell her fragrant hair, but the risk of arousal in such a public place, with the crowd still whirling about them, was far too dangerous.

'Where were you thinking of going?' she asked.

'Here,' he said firmly, pointing up the stairs, hoping there'd still be a table available. He started up a step and held out his hand.

Her eyes sparkled. 'Oh, *here*.' The thrilled note in her voice caught at his heart. 'Do you remember that night we had dinner here? You know…' she lowered her lashes and her voice faltered a little '…before?'

'I do remember,' he said steadily, holding her hand. 'I'll never forget it.'

'It should be excellent for doing some planning, don't you think?'

In Lara's view, Guillaume's was the most exciting restaurant in Sydney. Positioned in the southernmost shell of the Opera House, it had enormous windows facing the harbour, and more facing the city. With night craft glimmering on the water all around them, the Bridge and city towers a blaze of lights, it was easy to believe the restaurant was afloat.

And there was an excitement in the atmosphere, as if its glitzy clientele were as thrilled to be indulging themselves in fine wine and cuisine amidst the sophisticated decor as she was herself. It was a pity no one she knew from Newtown was present to see her walk in with the hottest marquis currently in Australia.

She and Alessandro were shown to a discreet booth angled to face the glittering night panorama on the harbour. Their table, swathed in white linen, gleamed with silver and crystal. She slipped off her pashmina and felt Alessandro's gaze on her throat and arms.

'Oh, dear.' She grinned, though she felt the warmth rise to her cheeks. 'Long tablecloths.'

Alessandro broke into a laugh, then he grew silent, the sensual hunger in his dark eyes stirring her, while the emotions of the day rose between them, twanging with the echoes of discord.

She indicated their window. 'Is it as good as your view of the Grand Canal?'

'Oh, sure, sure it is. Definitely. Absolutely.'

She laughed. 'Careful not to protest too much.'

They examined the wine list together, but the truth was Lara hardly needed wine this evening. With the excitement in her heart, she wasn't even sure she could eat.

She wondered where she would begin. She smiled and made her choices, conscious of how precious was this time with Alessandro, tense with the knowledge that it could all disappear in a few days.

She let her gaze rest on his beautiful, lean hands as they made an occasional eloquent gesture, and her confidence faltered. He led such a sophisticated life with his constant travel, his pleasure in the finer things, it was hard to imagine him embracing the nitty-gritty of child-raising.

'Dom Perignon, sir.'

Lara's eyes widened as the drinks waiter presented the distinctive bottle to Alessandro for inspection, then with a professional flourish removed the cork and decanted the foaming champagne without spilling a drop.

Alessandro picked up his glass. *'Salute.'*

'Wow.' The glasses clinked. 'What are we celebrating?'

His eyes smiled into hers, dark liquid fire. 'Finding each other again.'

Her insides surged in excited anticipation. The words augured well. She sipped the golden, sparkling liquid. The zing foamed through her bloodstream, or maybe it was Alessandro's shimmering, intent gaze.

'Delicious.' She sat back against the banquette, glass in hand. 'I'm so glad I ran into you tonight. I've been er—

thinking…' The warmth and sensuality of his gaze was so flattering, with his smile reflected in his eyes, it was hard to
catch her breath. She hoped she wasn't about to ruin everything by broaching the inflammatory subject. She hesitated,
then said with some constraint, 'I really appreciate your
thoughtfulness in what you suggested today. You were quite
right. About—deciding on a suitable location where you can
meet Vivi.'

His eyes sharpened, then veiled. But she could feel the
power of his attention like a high-voltage searchlight.

He lifted his shoulders. 'It seemed sensible.' But she could
tell he was pleased.

'Are you busy on Saturday?' She cast him a glance from
beneath her lashes. 'I thought it might be best if we introduced
you somewhere that's very familiar to her.'

'Not the schoolyard?'

'No, *not* the schoolyard.' She rolled her eyes. 'Heavens,
will I ever be able to walk in there again without blushing?'

'It's probably safer for us to save that location for ourselves.' His eyes gleamed. 'In the midnight hours.' He sipped
his wine, his eyes dwelling on her face. 'So you're thinking—
at your home? Mightn't that be a bit confronting?'

'Possibly. You may be right, that being her safe haven and
everything.' She gave her champagne a swirl. 'There is of
course the park. She knows it very well, and there's play
equipment there. If necessary she could play while we talk.'

'Ah, yes, now that sounds good. Does she—does she have
a lot to say?'

'When she's happy and comfortable she chatters like a
tree full of cockatoos.'

He smiled, and sat there thinking. 'Is there something else
we should do? Perhaps go on a trip, visit the zoo, or… What
do you suggest?'

'Why don't we see how it goes? If we get on, we might
make a plan for Sunday.'

His smile illuminated his entire face. '*Molto bene.* I will keep Sunday free.' He hesitated a moment. 'So…how will you tell her?'

'I told her about you this afternoon after we saw the flowers. And thank you for those, by the way. You must have been feeling very— They're gorgeous.'

He waved his hand. 'The least I could do. So… How did she—how did she take it?'

She smiled in recollection. 'Very matter-of-factly, actually.' She broke into a laugh. 'You're not quite up there with Santa Claus, but that's because she hasn't seen you yet. Once she meets you…' She lowered her lashes to conceal a sudden mistiness, and said huskily, 'Once she meets you, she will know.'

'What will she know?' he said softly.

'How—how you are.'

'And how is that?'

'Among other things—hot.'

He laughed and took her hand and kissed it. 'Thank you for the compliment. Likewise.'

She clasped fingers with him, savouring the warmth and strength of his firm grasp, a tremulous glow in her heart. She glanced at him. 'And there's something I must explain to you. About what happened six years ago.'

Though sitting quite still, he seemed to immobilise to an even deeper stillness, while his gaze grew darker and more unfathomable. She could sense a tension in his lean, lithe frame, and realised that everything she said now was in some way crucial.

'I'm sorry about today, Alessandro. Those things I said. Blaming you and shrieking at you like that in the lobby like a—a—when I know now it wasn't your fault, at all. I can't explain why those feelings all had to come boiling up again, after all this time. I'd thought they were all dead and buried. I guess because of the way I felt *then*— Although you know, I probably only felt the way *any* woman would feel, when I read you were married.' She lowered her gaze, then glanced up at him. 'The truth is, I really intended to meet you at Centrepoint that day.'

His eyes sharpened in incredulity. *'Cosa?'*

She nodded. 'I was all ready to go with you. Suitcase packed and all. And I would have, except that I was in hospital at the time.'

He swivelled his body around to face her in full. *'Per carità.* In hospital? Why was that?'

Despite her resolve to stay calm, when she saw his concerned expression she felt the tears well in her throat. 'I told you about the summer of the bushfires. Well, that was the summer.'

'You mean—*that* summer? When your father died?'

'Yes, *that* summer. After we made that pact…' His jaw hardened, and he drew breath to speak, but she waved her hand to prevent him. 'My fault, I know, I know. If you only knew how much I regret it…' Her voice started to tremble. She snapped open her purse for a bunch of tissues, and wiped her nose, then took a further moment to calm herself.

He hastened in with, 'No, no, please, don't be upset.' He added, a little stiffly, 'I know— I may have said some things about that pact. Perhaps I sounded negative. Well, it *was* an outrageous demand, wasn't it, an absolutely incredible test of a man's—!' He broke off and breathed rather hard for some seconds. *'But…'* He recovered his composure and threw up his hands. 'I have to accept that I did agree to it. In the end.' His lips tightened. 'Against my better judgement.'

She winced. 'I'm sorry. I had no idea at the time that you felt so strongly about it. But you know, I was quite *young*. I didn't know you all that well…'

He stemmed her defences with a hasty gesture. 'All right, yes, yes, I know, I know. Let's not dwell too much on the whys and wherefors, now. So…' His brilliant dark gaze was intent on her face. 'What happened?'

She was silent for a moment, gathering her thoughts. 'Well,

after you left, I worked out my notice in my job. Then I gave up my flat and travelled up to Bindinong to spend the final week with my parents. There'd been fires around, as there are every summer. But with the weather conditions a few days before I was due to meet you it all suddenly exploded out of control. This huge fire swept down from the ridge and right through the town. Our street was cut off, and our house went up along with some others. Dad and I and a few other people were trapped. Most of us survived, only Dad...'

Even thinking of it brought back the choking smell of smoke, the fearful roaring of a world engulfed in flame, the searing, terrifying heat. Her throat closed and she broke off and allowed a gesture to take the place of words. Alessandro leaned across and took her arms, stroking her and making concerned, soothing murmurs.

When she could speak again, she said, 'I was one of the lucky ones. The Fire Service got me out.'

'But you were injured?'

She glanced at him, hesitating. 'Oh, well, I had—you know, a bump on the head. What they call a little hairline fracture, and a small, insignificant—burn...' Conscious of his fixed, querying gaze, she steeled herself to lift her hair. Ignoring her drumming heart, she flashed him a glimpse of the scar running down her nape to her shoulder.

He gave a sharp exclamation. She risked a glance at him, and saw that his dark eyes looked stricken. Though perhaps not with the horror she'd dreaded. And not revulsion either, apparently, to her extreme relief. It seemed to be more concern and sympathy he was feeling, because he put his arms around her and kissed her forehead, then her cheeks, then her lips with the most fervent tenderness.

'Oh, Lara,' he said thickly. 'My poor Larissa. If only I had known this. If only...' His arms tightened around her and she responded in kind, hugging him, pressing her lips to his strong neck, enjoying the wonderful masculine scents of him and the feel of his powerful heartbeat, thundering away next to hers. 'How long were you in the hospital, *tesoro*?'

'A couple of weeks. It took me a few days to wake up.'

'*Per carità.* You could have *died.*'

'Oh, no. Heavens, I was lucky. Look, this is *nothing*,' she said when he finally released her, to her intense regret. Well, he had to. They were in a public restaurant, and after *last* night there were definite risks. Even under such teary conditions she felt pleasantly stimulated by the contact with his big, warm body.

'A little scarring, is all,' she went on, dismissing it with an airy gesture. 'Compared to what some people suffered it's— minuscule. A bagatelle.' He reached to lift her hair for another inspection, but she moved sharply aside. 'No, don't. Please.'

Comprehension gleamed in his dark eyes, and he grew contrite. 'I'm—sorry.' Then he added, his face a little stiff, 'I am—I am *devastated* by all of this, *tesoro*, but in some way so relieved to *know*.' His hands lifted as if he needed to touch her, grab her, but he put them down again. 'It changes every-thing. To know that at least you tried to…' He bunched his fists. 'If only I had known *sooner*.' He sat back against the banquette, shaking his head and exclaiming in Italian. After a few seconds he glanced enquiringly at her. 'You mentioned that fire the other night, but I never connected it. You should have explained.'

'Should I?' She made a slight grimace. 'You hadn't been so very pleased to see me earlier, though, had you? I guess I felt—wary of saying too much.'

'Ah.' He looked remorseful and lifted his shoulders in ac-knowledgement. 'When I saw your name on that list the first day, I admit it was a shock. I wasn't sure how I would feel about seeing you. But…' he exhaled a long breath '…I under-stand now.' He turned sharply to rake her with a serious gaze. 'And—when did you find out you were pregnant?'

She grimaced. 'In the hospital.'

He closed his eyes. 'Oh. How it must have been for you.

What you have suffered… You and your mother. Losing your poor father…'

'I admit it *was* hard at first.' She gave a rueful shrug. 'But we're over it now, and we're fine. *Really.*' She met his gaze fleetingly, conscious of his intent scrutiny. 'The first year or two were pretty challenging, but, you know, life goes on. Even the worst grief softens. We made it through the bad time.' She glanced at him and said softly, 'Well, you know, we had Vivi to live for.'

He met her gaze, a warm shimmer lighting his eyes.

The waiter appeared again and swooped down with the selection of small dishes of fragrant, steaming delicacies.

Alessandro dealt with him with his usual courtesy, but his expression was serious and distracted. As soon as the man was out of earshot, he turned to her with more avid questions, about that time in hospital, her recovery, her ability to communicate.

'Everything the Meadows family owned was lost,' she explained. 'My phone, et cetera, with your number in it.' She shook her head in wry remembrance. 'You'd have thought yours would be *one* number I'd remember, but for weeks after the event it was as if my brain was paralysed. I could hardly remember my own name. It was the trauma of the blow mixed with the shock, they said.'

'Well, that certainly explains why I couldn't make any connection when I phoned you. *Dio*, how frustrated I was.' He took up the servers and spooned some truffled tortellini with lobster sauce onto her plate. 'Would I be right in guessing that later on when you'd recovered enough to try you couldn't find me?'

She nodded. 'When I phoned Harvard, the university refused to release any information. Finally, after about the tenth call, someone told me you were no longer a student there. I felt so… I didn't know *where* you were in the world. Where to look.' She grimaced. 'And I really *needed* to find you, of course…'

She paused and, drawing another preparatory breath, heard Alessandro cursing softly to himself.

'Oh, fool that I was. And then you learned of my marriage.'

She shrugged and smiled at him through her mist. 'I might as well admit that back then, I was—in love with you, I suppose. Well…' She cast him a sidelong glance. 'I was much younger then, I'd had no experience of sophisticated affairs with citizens of the world. So when I saw about your—your wedding…in that magazine…' Her throat swelled at the remembered pain.

He sighed. 'If I had only known this. I could have…I could have— Everything would have been different.'

'Would it?' She swallowed. 'Oh, well. It's all water under the bridge now.' She shrugged and raised rueful eyes to his. 'Call it Fate, or whatever. And when I think of what *you* must have gone through when you came to meet me and I wasn't there… Oh, poor Sandro, I'm so, so sorry. What you must have thought… And all these years I've been thinking such harsh things about you.'

He looked rueful, and in the muted light of the restaurant she thought she could detect a faint flush under his olive tan. He made a small grimace. '*You* have thought harsh things.'

With a stab of remorse she bit her lip, reaching to take his hand again. 'Oh, of *course* you must have felt like that, of course. Flying all that way and thinking I'd let you down. Oh, that ridiculous pact. I'm so ashamed to have insisted on it. Why did you ever agree?' She caught his darkening gaze and quickly moved the conversation on. 'And I understand now.' She looked at him through her lashes. 'This is why you were so hostile the other day. No *wonder*. Who could ever blame you?'

He took immediate issue with her reading. 'I wouldn't say *hostile*. I may have been—reserved. I needed to—consider the situation.'

A silence fell while she considered the implications of everything. All her misconceptions had suddenly turned themselves around to stand the right way up.

She glanced at him. 'Is—that why you said you had

nothing to lose? When you—married Giulia? Because you felt—let down?'

He frowned, then lifted his shoulders and said in a gruff voice, 'There may have been—some sort of rebound response in my thinking at the time.'

She looked wonderingly at him, her over-full heart fluttering in her chest like a cricket. 'So—you *did* want me, back then?'

He gazed at her for a long intense moment, while her pulse rushed faster than a white-water torrent, and said very quietly, 'I think I must have.' Then his mouth relaxed and his eyes lit with an ironic gleam. 'Well, I *was* quite young.'

Her heart skipped a few bars and she put her trembling hands to her cheeks. 'It's all so unbelievable, I can hardly think straight. I think we'll both need time to process it all.'

Despite his gently mocking response, the air felt suddenly charged with questions. If he'd truly wanted her *then*, did that mean he would now? One thing was certain. Despite his reserve she could sense a burning turbulence behind his lean, intelligent face, as though her revelation had detonated a major realignment of his ideas. Maybe it was as cataclysmic as the one she was experiencing herself.

His dark eyes scanned her face, then he leaned across and kissed her lips. 'What you need now is to eat some of this delicious little supper, and then I think we should walk.'

She smiled. 'Walk where?'

'To the Seasons,' he said firmly.

CHAPTER SIXTEEN

IN A few short days, the world had changed, Alessandro marvelled to himself as he hustled Lara the few tree-lined blocks past Circular Quay and into George Street. Soon he would meet his daughter, his own flesh and blood.

He contemplated that shining truth, his heart filled to bursting with the miracle of it. Why had he ever found it so threatening?

He cringed to think of his behaviour to Lara that first night. That whole first *day*.

He grilled her with questions about the hardships she'd faced as a single parent, possessed of a burning need to make up for it all and show her what was in his heart. Unfortunately, the English language, excellent as it was, lacked the versatility of Italian when it came to expressing such powerful emotions, and a man could hardly sing in a Sydney street. There was only one true way he could be sure of.

Fortunately, the short walk to the Seasons was peppered with shadowy nooks and crannies. Perfect for a man eager to demonstrate his gratitude and affection to a woman without causing her public embarrassment.

Once or twice, laughing, he swept her into the shadows, dragged her into his arms and kissed her until her sweet, shuddering breath mingled with his, and she trembled and panted for more. Once he kissed her so ruthlessly, so thoroughly, none of the secret, thrilling places of her supple body escaped his bold, marauding hands.

By the time he inserted the room key into the lock, he was hard, and he could sense her desire as tangibly as his own. Her eyes were the dark, smoky blue that turned his blood into molten lava.

Inside the softly lit room, her initial reticence the previous evening, with her shy request to dim the lights, flooded back to him, poignant with a meaning that twisted his heart. But his instincts for what was right asserted themselves. There would be no more secrets between them. No forbidden areas.

He took her in his arms, and she linked hers around his neck in captivating compliance while he backed her towards the bed with a kiss.

'Now,' he said, gently removing her pashmina.

On the edge of a heavenly suspense, Lara surrendered to the electric pleasure of his touch as he stroked her hair back from her forehead, and traced the line of her cheekbones with his finger.

'You are just as I remember you that very first time.' Desire darkened his eyes, his voice. 'Still so beautiful.'

'Not quite, I'm afraid.' She made a wry little grimace.

His dark eyes filled with ardent tenderness. 'More so, *tesoro*,' he said fiercely, his voice thickening. 'Even more.'

He drew her to the bed, and she sat beside him while he yanked off his shoes and socks. Then he reached under her hair for the zip on her dress and drew it down. She felt cool air on her bare back, and felt his supple fingers trace the ridge of her spine all the way to her nape, then pause to linger at one point, before reversing to trace the scar where it slewed across her shoulder.

She tensed and would have jerked away, but he murmured, 'No, don't flinch.'

She sat very still, forcing herself not to react. Not to shy away from his sure touch, although her insides were clenched in a knot.

The scar was smooth after all this time, but it had a different smoothness from the surrounding skin, almost a slippery, satin feel. Trembling, she felt his fingers trace the shape of it, all the way up her nape and into her hair. He pushed the hair aside.

He must have been able to see the puckered skin quite clearly, yet he didn't shudder away, or show disgust. She sat bolt upright, her breath coming in tiny shallow gasps as she stared at the carpet and tried to dissociate. A tremor rocked her when, to her absolute shock, she felt him bend and press his lips to the damaged tissue. He continued, kissing the entire length of the scar, up into her hair and back again. After the first paralysed moments, she closed her eyes, willing herself not to shudder and flinch, and gradually allowed the knot inside her to dissolve.

She could sense no diminishment in his desire, rather it felt like the reverse. The simmering heat emanating from him escalated as his lips traversed her shoulder. Then with passionate hunger he turned her to him and kissed her throat, and her face.

The dress slipped off her shoulders, and he bent his lips to her breasts and unfastened her bra.

After that, there was no place for anxiety. There were only Alessandro's hands and lips, the rough skin of his jaw and cheek on her smooth, naked breasts, the passion storming her veins.

He undressed her with hot, urgent hands, then stripped off his own clothes, pushing her before him onto the bed with a deep, possessive kiss.

She lay beside him, thrilling while he explored her nude body with his tongue and clever fingers, passion smouldering in his dark eyes.

He lit trails of fire in her skin, softly tickled the sensitive petals beneath the blonde triangle he found so beautiful, first with his fingers, then his tongue, fanning the flames of her desire until she moaned and panted in a wanton frenzy of restless need.

He moved over her, positioning himself between her

thighs. He gazed down at her, his eyes serious and intense. His voice was as dark as if it came from the depths of him. 'Do you know how I felt when you weren't there? I had— nowhere in the world I wanted to be. I felt—such a terrible emptiness. It was like they say. Your heart breaks.'

There was a hoarseness in his voice that moved her to the core of her being. His dark eyes were sincere, his lean, strong face working with emotion.

Remorse and love swelled in her heart. She put her arms around him and held him close to her, his heart beating against hers.

She kissed him, and his response was so fierce, so passion- ate, the pure clear flame of lust rose in her. She arched under him, opening her legs and inviting him in for the slow, sensual ride to rapture. She rocked him in her arms while he thrust his hard shaft into her moist sheath, stroking her inside walls until the pleasure roared to a giddy pinnacle and spasmed in waves of ecstasy.

Later on, she rode him, relishing the sexy slide of his velvet hardness inside her slick channel, enjoying the ripple of muscle under his bronzed skin, loving the contrast of her smooth softness with his lean angularity. She thrilled when he flipped her over onto her back, and with athletic thorough- ness, brought her to another fantastic climax.

Towards dawn, sated, supple and replete, Alessandro gath- ered her into the curve of his body, her firm, warm buttocks pressed deliciously against his groin, and fell deeply asleep. His dreams were a heavenly bliss of languorous blue eyes, enticing him to love. Shapely limbs and silken skin, sliding against his. Smooth, pale breasts with nipples taut enough to make his tongue water, their peach-hued areola a miracle of delicate beauty.

Something roused him from his dream state. He opened his eyes. Feeling a coldness, he dragged himself up on his elbow. The pale light of dawn was streaming through the windows.

He blinked. Why weren't the drapes drawn? After a second his eyes focused on Lara, fully dressed, tiptoeing to the door.

'*Per carità,*' he growled. 'What now? Where are you going?'

She arrested in her tracks and turned with a rueful grin. 'I'm sorry, darling, I have to go. I really have to. Vivi will be awake any minute now. I have to be there. This is how it is when you're a parent. Sorry.'

She blew him a kiss.

The door clicked shut, and she was gone.

CHAPTER SEVENTEEN

SATURDAY dawned fine and clear, with a snappy little breeze scurrying dead leaves along the Newtown pavements. Lara had left it until the morning of the day to tell Vivi they were meeting Alessandro, in case Vivi worried about it.

Lara was nervous enough for the both of them. Unsure she was up to the emotions of such a significant event, she could hardly settle to one thing.

Greta had gone on one of her weekend jaunts with her amateur orchestra, so Lara and Vivi had the entire house to themselves. Lara made the low-key announcement to Vivi during breakfast, not wanting to make it sound like the most momentous occasion of the past five years.

She wasn't sure how well she succeeded. Vivi gazed back at her over her porridge, her dark eyes wide and curious, and perhaps a bit wary.

'Is he your husband?' she asked after a long suspense-ful minute.

'No, no,' Lara said. 'He's—a friend. You'll see. A very nice friend.'

Alessandro took a long early morning run around the fore-shore in the bracing air, blind to the sights and scents of the harbour traffic, his breath coming in foggy puffs. White horses tossed on the waves, the wintry sun lending them a chill sparkle, though he barely noticed.

What did a man say to a small girl? He should have checked with Lara, had something suitable prepared.

He'd bought Vivi a heart-shaped pendant locket, with delicate filigree and a tiny inset ruby, on an incredibly fine gold chain. Too much? he wondered. Should he have checked with Lara about that?

Showering after the run, he took extra care shaving. He didn't want to scare his daughter into thinking he was some big, rough, hairy creature. For a second he paused in scraping away foam to grin, reflecting that her mother didn't seem to object to those aspects of him.

Dressed casually in blue jeans, a polo shirt and loafers, he embarked on his room-service breakfast, then pushed it aside. Coffee was enough.

The meeting was set for eleven to give Vivi just enough time to get used to the idea, but not too much.

He located the park ahead of the appointed time, drawing the car up under the boughs of a massive Moreton Bay fig. Conscious of his quickened pulse, he got out, then strolled in under the trees, choosing what looked like a promising walk to take him through to the duck pond. Other people were about, parents, children, but he hardly absorbed their presence. How absurd, that one small girl could make a man's heart tremble.

At a bend in the path he stopped still, a sharp lurch in his chest.

Ahead in a wide clearing he saw Lara, standing at the edge of a pond with a little dark-haired girl, indicating something in the water. The child was gazing in, looking up to her mother to speak, then pointing into the water.

His daughter. His heart made a fierce escalation.

As though sensing his presence Lara glanced around and saw him. She bent to speak to the child, and he saw Vivi turn sharply his way and reach for her mother's hand.

After a small hesitation they advanced, and he moved forward to meet them, a tumultuous recognition surging in him as the small solemn face grew closer and more distinct.

Her features were as delicate as her mother's, though her colouring was his own. She was dressed in miniature jeans and a pink fleecy top with butterflies dancing across it.

Lara felt Vivi's hand tighten in hers and forced her own legs to keep on walking, though every kind of flying insect was fluttering through her insides and her limbs were all at once composed of sponge rubber.

Alessandro walked up to them with his long easy stride, seemingly cool and assured, and stirringly handsome in blue jeans and a black leather jacket.

Lara exchanged greetings with him while Vivi stayed attached to her side. It was a surreal moment. She felt torn, the immediate, almost tangible current of desire and connection with her lover at war with her closeness to her child.

She saw Alessandro's dark gaze sweep from her to Vivi, and with a surprised pang registered uncertainty in his smile. She pulled herself together to take charge.

'Darling,' she said, smiling down at Vivi, 'this is Alessandro.'

Alessandro crouched down to speak to Vivi at her level, his dark eyes shining with a tenderness that brought a lump to Lara's throat. 'And what is your name?'

Vivi's big, soft dark eyes gazed shyly at him in return, then she murmured, 'Vivienne Alessandra Meadows.'

Alessandro's lashes flickered, then for an instant his gaze met Lara's, the shimmer in his eyes causing hers to moisten.

'Ah,' he said, smiling at Vivi, 'now that—that is a very beautiful name.' Though his deep gentle voice held steady, Lara could detect his emotion and it further destabilised her own rocky control.

'See, I have brought something for you.' He reached into his pocket and brought out a small pink velvet case.

Vivi looked at it with wondering eyes, then glanced up at Lara.

Lara smiled through her mist. 'Go on. It's for you. You can take it.'

The case was solemnly accepted, and, with some rather clumsy help from Lara, who had to blink rapidly so she could see well enough, opened to reveal the exquisite little treasure within. Vivi gazed speechlessly at it.

'Thank you,' Lara whispered to Vivi with a nudge. Vivi's lips moved, but no sound came out.

'Would you like to put it on?' Lara persevered.

Vivi shook her head, but when Lara offered to carry the case for her the offer was firmly rejected. Alessandro rose to his feet.

There was a small silence. Alessandro turned away and put on his sunglasses.

Lara stepped in to ease the moment on. 'It's chilly, isn't it? I'm glad there's some sunshine, at least.'

Alessandro turned back to them with a smile, his deep voice a little rough around the edges. 'Isn't there always sunshine in Australia?' He looked at Vivi. 'It doesn't ever rain here, does it, Vivi?'

Vivi preferred not to say. She clung tight to Lara's hand, and stared very interestedly at a spot on the ground. Conversation came to a standstill.

'Well,' Lara said brightly, 'I feel like a walk. Don't you, Alessandro? Why don't we go and see what the ducks are doing now? I've a strong suspicion there are eels lurking in that pond.'

'Eels! Well, now, eels are exactly what I feel like seeing right now,' Alessandro said, flashing her a grateful grin. 'And after that, I would like to find out if there are any swings here in this park.'

That was too much for Vivi. 'There *are* some swings,' she ventured to murmur from the safety of Lara's side. 'And a slippery slide.'

By the time the ducks had been re-examined, and a suspect eel had been spotted and exclaimed over, and Vivi had taken a dozen slides with not one, but *two* parents eager to catch her and save her from falling in the inevitable puddle at the bottom—not that Alessandro's offers were ever accepted—a thaw had set in.

Lara suggested that Alessandro should come home with them for lunch. Alessandro accepted at once, declaring he was so hungry he could eat an elephant, causing Vivi to exchange a shocked glance with her mother. But she skipped excitedly along with them on the way to the car, and when, at Lara's instructions, they stopped at a deli in King Street to buy some delicacies, she was by turn horrified and fascinated at Alessandro's choices.

'I don't eat anchovies,' she told him with grave disapproval. 'And I don't eat artichokes.'

'Do you eat olives?' he said.

She shook her head.

'Ah, but one day you will. You will see.'

'No, I won't.'

She was quite firm also on the possibility of ever being brought to eat prosciutto, pastrami, or sardines wrapped in bacon and served on mozzarella toast with basil.

Lunch was a great success, to Lara's relief. Alessandro was as hungry as he'd promised, and by the time he'd shocked Vivi to the core by drizzling olive oil on his bread and cleaning up everything everyone else didn't eat she relaxed enough to ask him if he would like to see Kylie Minogie.

'Kylie Minogie?' he echoed, looking mystified.

Lara lilted her eyebrows to signal the austere honour he was being granted, so he gravely assented to being very wishful of meeting that person. When Vivi skipped from her bedroom importantly bearing her beloved doll, Lara had to restrain a laugh at Alessandro's faintly bemused expression.

But he made a swift recovery. 'Oh, of course,' he said smoothly. 'Kylie Minogie. Well, well, Kylie. Aren't you beautiful?'

Though Kylie had lost a great deal of her hair and was looking a bit the worse for wear, he allowed her to perch on his knee while the tea was being poured. Vivi stared with such fascination at Kylie's exalted position, Lara suspected she might have been a little envious. She was rather envious herself.

After the lunch had been cleared, Vivi made several trips to retrieve treasures for Alessandro's approval, including every photo taken of the Meadows family since she was born, until Lara was laughingly forced to call a halt.

'Poor Alessandro looks tired,' she told Vivi. 'He needs a rest now.'

Alessandro's eyes gleamed with amusement. 'I am a little tired. Maybe I should lie down on your bed, Mummy. What do you think?'

'Oh, we can do better than that for you,' she said, smiling. 'How about a walk?'

Alessandro's brows went up and his devil's smile flashed. 'It would have to be a very good walk. Ah, I know. How about a drive *and* a walk?'

To Vivi's great excitement, he drove them to Bondi, where he and Lara played chasing games with her until Lara collapsed on the sand, feigning exhaustion. Alessandro dropped down beside her, and they watched while Vivi investigated the treasures to be found at the water's edge, swooping down on shells, squealing with delight every time an icy little wave rushed far enough up the beach to splash her bare feet.

'Simple pleasures provide such endless delight,' Alessandro observed, slipping his arm around Lara and kissing her ear. 'So this is what it's like being a parent.'

'This is what it's like,' she acknowledged. 'Full on, day and night. No looking away.'

For a long time he was silent, frowning a little, his chiselled profile brooding against the lengthening rays of the sun.

Lara's fear, never far below the surface, stirred to gnaw at her precarious happiness.

What was he thinking? Was he feeling daunted? Looking

forward with relief to that plane he'd be boarding at the end of the week?

'That's—a very lovely gift you gave her,' she ventured after a while. Unable to help herself, she said softly, 'Something for her to remember you by?'

He turned and his acute dark eyes shimmered into hers. 'For her to remember this *day* by,' he corrected gently.

CHAPTER EIGHTEEN

ALESSANDRO stayed for dinner. To Vivi's astonishment he insisted on being the cook, with Lara acting as his willing kitchen hand.

'Better a kitchen hand than a kitchen slave,' Lara murmured, inciting a wicked surmise in Alessandro's eyes. Then after dinner, when Vivi was fast asleep, though he'd intended to return to his hotel, desire swept them away and it seemed natural he should stay the night in Lara's bed.

By Sunday evening he was a shining prince in Vivi's eyes, and in her loving little heart as well, Lara could see. And who could blame her? What female could resist being charmed by the Marquis of the Venetian Isles?

Although Vivi was anxious he should stay to dinner again on Sunday, and for ever, as far as Lara could guess, as the day progressed Alessandro became increasingly quiet and pensive. Then late in the afternoon he informed them gently that he needed to go back to his hotel and prepare for the week to come.

It made sense to Lara, who had preparations of her own to take care of. But Vivi was disappointed, and so was she, in truth. She'd indulged herself in a daydream that, having come to visit once, Alessandro would never leave. She smiled goodbye, a tear in her heart when he bent to kiss Vivi, who reached up and put her arms around his neck.

In the morning at work, Alessandro called her into his office. Dressed in his business suit, once again he'd assumed that indefinable aura of the boss, even though he was her lover, and the father of her child. That didn't stop him from kissing her, however.

When the kiss ended he said, 'There's something I have to tell you.'

The ominous words sparked a pang of anxiety in Lara, but she concealed it with a grin. 'You're not pregnant?'

He smiled. 'Not this time.' He glanced cautiously at her and said, 'I'm flying back to Italy this evening.'

'What?' Shock made her numb. Her knees lost strength, and to her shame her voice wobbled. She could see the end of her golden time, the last precious, joyous day draining away.

But what had she expected? He'd made no promises to her except for one of Vivi's financial support. There was no commitment. She'd had hopes of one soon, but now…

Her disappointment was bitter. 'Oh. Already? Didn't you say—I thought—aren't you staying on until it's time to go to—to Bangkok?'

'I was, but circumstances have changed. But—don't look like that. There's no need for you to worry, *tesoro*.' He drew her back into his arms. 'I know it sounds sudden, but there are some urgent things I have to do there. It will only be for a few days. I'll probably call into Bangkok on the way back.'

She looked doubtfully at him. 'Really? On the way back *here*?'

'Yes, here. Really. I'm coming back.'

His eyes were so warm and sincere, but as she gazed searchingly at him his brows edged together. 'I *am* coming back,' he said in some exasperation. 'Don't you believe me?'

'All right. If you say so.' But her mind was working rapidly. What if, once he arrived in that other world, circumstances changed again and he was delayed long enough for her and Vivi to recede from his mind? He mightn't come back for months. Even a year. Her heart chilled. Vivi would have no closure. That goodbye yesterday might be the last for a very long time. Were two days with Vivi enough to cement her image in his heart for ever?

She tried to recover her poise and behave like an adult. 'What time is your flight? We'll come to the airport.'

He looked taken aback. 'Are you sure? There's no need to go to that inconvenience. What about Vivi's dinner? I'll be seeing you both again very soon.'

'There's every need,' she said firmly. 'Forget about her dinner. Vivi needs to say goodbye.'

In truth, six years hadn't made Lara any better at farewells. She tried to keep a smile for Vivi's sake, but when Alessandro held her fiercely against his chest and kissed her for the last time, tears rolled down her face, just like before. And when he picked Vivi up in his arms and kissed her, Lara could barely restrain herself from sobbing aloud.

'I'll phone you,' he said, his deep voice gruff and gentle at the same time. 'I promise.'

They watched him stride down the immigration corridor until he was out of sight, then turned away, despair in Lara's heart, at least. Vivi was too young to anticipate heartbreak.

Her mother wasn't so sanguine.

'It's a crying shame,' Greta said later that evening. 'He was such a nice lad. I had great hopes of him.'

'He *is* coming back, Mum.'

Greta looked grave. 'Oh, right. If you say so. Good.' She didn't sound very confident, and Lara's hopes sank deeper. Why hadn't he been keen on them saying farewell at the airport? Had he wanted to make a quick, clean getaway? No tears, no reproaches? No *conscience*?

At work she went through the motions like an automaton.

'Get a grip, honey,' Tuila said, stopping by her desk. 'He'll be back. He still hasn't found an MD. As if he's even...'

'Even what?' Lara enquired.

'Nothing. Forget I said a thing.'

But what did she say? Lara wondered.

'That guy's on a Formula One ride to nowhere fast,' Tuila muttered.

On Wednesday evening the phone rang during dinner. Lara's heart leaped up in hope, as it did every time a phone rang, and this time she wasn't disappointed.

'Hello, *tesoro*.' From across the world Alessandro's deep voice thrilled down her spine like dark melted chocolate. 'What are you doing right now?'

Beaming. Thrilling. Feeling my heart fly over the moon. 'Eating dinner with my family. What are *you* doing?'

'Ah, pity. I was going to ask you next what you are wearing. So—is Vivi there?'

'She is. And she's listening to every word.'

She could hear the smile in his voice. 'Good. She will keep me on the straight and narrow. Tell her her papa misses her. Do you have your passport?'

'What?'

'I want you to fly to me in Bangkok. Will you do it, Larissa?'

'Well, I had a passport, but it was… And I—you know I can't leave Vivi.'

'I don't want you to leave her. *Bring* her. Will you come, *tesoro*?'

'But…' Anxiety, joy and excitement seized her all at the same time. 'When? How—long for?'

'Two weeks. Three weeks. Until we're tired of the island life.'

'The *island life*,' she exclaimed.

'Yes. All three of us. So? Will you come?' There was a sudden urgency in his voice. 'Larissa?'

She looked at Vivi and her mother, both avidly staring at her trying to make sense of the conversation, and her heart bounded in her chest with a joyful, rock-solid certainty.

She seized the moment.

'Yes, Sandro. We'll come.'

* * *

Touchdown. As the big machine roared into the ground-wind on the tarmac and gradually reduced velocity Lara unclenched every muscle in her body and allowed herself to breathe out. Whew, thank heavens for that.

Vivi stirred. Their air-beds had been folded away long since, but Vivi had dropped off to sleep again in her seat. All around people started shuffling, relaxing as the plane slowed, though the lights still warned them to keep their seat belts fastened. Lara smiled at Vivi and patted her reassuringly, then dived for her capacious bag and checked it for the umpteenth time. Money, passports, hotel confirmation, sunglasses, tissues, Kylie…

The airport was a breeze. Huge, space-age and remarkably easy to navigate for the unseasoned traveller. With Vivi clutching her hand, Lara managed to queue through immigration and retrieve her suitcase, her tremulous excitement mounting with every second. Would he be there?

She and Vivi were waved through Customs unhindered. Emerging into the main concourse, Lara scanned until her eager gaze was captured by a tall, lean, darkly handsome man strolling towards them. As her teary gaze locked with his long stride quickened, then he broke into a run.

He caught both of them in his arms, kissing Vivi, then holding Lara so tight against his chest she could scarcely breathe.

'Was it terrible?' He kissed her ruthlessly. 'Were you afraid, *tesoro mio*? You were so brave to come. And you, Vivi. Did you sleep? Did you look after your mummy for me?'

After a while of relishing being crushed against his big iron-hard frame and enjoying his clean masculine scent, Lara became conscious that they were blocking one of the exits, and her linen jacket and trousers were in danger of being wrinkled.

With a shaky laugh she disentangled herself from the really quite stimulating embrace.

Some air hosties strolling by, elegantly towing their neat little suitcases, swept Alessandro with admiring glances and raised artfully shaped brows at her. Lara could have sworn she recognised a couple of them from that terrace in Roseleigh Avenue.

She grinned, drew herself up and took Alessandro's arm. 'Come, darling.'

Outside the terminal, Alessandro steered them to a waiting limousine while the driver dealt with their bags. Lara and Vivi wilted in a wave of heat to match anything Sydney could turn on in the height of summer. There was no patch of blue. A red angry ball burned through a heavy, sultry haze of smog.

As Alessandro settled them into the car Lara felt grateful for having changed Vivi and herself into cooler clothes.

'Tonight we sleep here in Bangkok,' Alessandro said, 'then tomorrow we fly to an island.'

Vivi's eyes widened. 'An island.'

'Yes, Vivi. An island with white sand and coral, and pretty fish and boats, and the gentlest people on earth.' He narrowed his eyes in thought. 'I think there might even be monkeys not too far away.'

'*Monkeys.*'

He laughed and kissed her, then reached for Lara's hand. 'How I've missed this.'

Lara gave him a rueful grin. 'You'll get used to our charms pretty fast, I'm afraid, *signor.*'

'That's exactly the point, *carissima.*'

In the evening of a very long day, which had involved sailing to a beach where monkeys performed audacious and disconcerting acts of mischief on unwary visitors, Alessandro strolled to where Lara was lounging on the verandah of their thatched island home, dreamily gazing out to sea.

He handed her a long, cool, pink drink, then dropped down on the lounger beside her, stretching out his bare, bronzed legs, and leaning back on the cushions.

'She's fast asleep.' His deep voice was rich with satisfaction.

'Monkeys can be very tiring,' Lara observed, resting her hand on a muscular, hairy thigh.

He gave a husky laugh. 'We must remember that in future.'

Lara slanted him a smiling glance. 'I did warn you.'

'Yes, you did. But I could never have imagined how fantastic the reality would be.'

'No, really?'

He kissed her. 'Yes, *really*.'

Alessandro had missed shaving that morning, and the dark shadow of his beard gave him a devilish, piratical charm Lara found hard to overlook.

She was silent for a while, listening to the gentle swish and fall of the waves on the beach, dwelling on the supreme happiness of being with a beautiful sexy man who could cook.

'You know, *carissa*, I've been thinking.'

She lifted her brows.

'Those MDs we looked at for Stiletto were bloody hopeless.'

'All of them?'

'Yes, all. They were all too young, too—too— Half of them looked like *cricketers*.'

She stared at him in surprise. 'Is that a bad thing?'

He gazed at her with narrowed eyes and said austerely, 'We can do better.'

She took a sip. 'Sounds as if you have someone in mind.' She glanced at him, and her heart made a wild bounce. 'Aha. You're not by any chance thinking…'

'I am thinking it. It would do that workforce good to have a serious shake-up. How can I trust one of these cowboys to do it? So…' he twirled a lock of her hair around his finger and gave it a little tweak '…that was one of the reasons I needed to fly to Italia. There were arrangements to be made.'

She sat bolt upright. 'Oh, but that's—*wonderful*. So you'll be staying in Sydney for a while?' She gazed at him, her heart in her throat, all her irrepressible hopes and dreams rushing madly to the surface.

'I would like to.' He smiled and it crept into his dark eyes. 'I was thinking—until Vivi is finished primary school, at least. Then we might reconsider, if necessary. Half of her heritage is in Europe. I would like her to know the rest of her family. We'll see how we go. In the meantime, we can take holidays…exchange visits…'

'Oh.' Visions of holidays in Venice whirling through her head couldn't for the moment compete with the one blissful fact. 'So…you're staying—with *us*? Definitely staying?'

He lowered his gaze, and when he looked up again his eyes were serious and grave. '*Where* I stay in Sydney— depends on one thing.' He took her hands in his firm, light grasp, and took a few seconds to arrange the words. 'I am so in love with you, Lara. I was hoping, if we spent this little time here, you might feel that the three of us could be together all the time.'

'Oh.' Joyful tears sprang into her eyes and she said softly, 'Sandro, you must know I love you. There's nothing I would like more.'

His dark eyes lit with a warm, tender glow that matched the joy in her heart. She bent to press her lips to his, and his arm slid around her as he responded with a delicious enthusiasm. After a good long while he broke the tingling connection and set her a little away from him.

'No, no, don't tempt me,' he said, his breathing as ragged as her own. 'Not yet. Not until we get some things straightened out.'

He changed position so they were both propped comfortably up against the cushions.

His expression was suddenly grave. 'There is one thing on my mind, *tesoro*.' He hesitated. 'Call me a throwback to mediaeval times, but I do observe some obligations to my family.' All at once he looked quite stern, like a proud, darkly handsome pirate captain reviewing the past that had shaped his aristocratic heritage. 'The Vincentis can be flexible about most traditions, but one of them is really quite—uncompromising.'

'Oh?' She felt a sudden chill of excitement. A delicious, anticipatory buzz warmed her veins.

He took her hand and kissed it. 'It's a small thing, *carissima*. We Vincentis like to marry our women. It might be seen as an old-fashioned practice in some places, perhaps, but—' he shrugged '—it is—still important to me.' He dropped a light kiss on her nose and grinned. 'There isn't much point being a *marchese* if you can't persuade some woman to be your *marchesa*.'

She laughed. 'I can't believe you haven't had heaps of offers.'

His eyes glinted. 'There've been—one or two who might have been willing. Too willing, in fact. Neither of them was the one.'

'The one? I know what you mean. No one else will do. And if others are too willing—what a turn-off.'

'Exactly.' He smiled. 'Now, take your case. I've had such a hard time catching you, *tesoro,* I feel I need to pin you down. Somehow, I feel I need to know we are truly together. That it's permanent.' He flashed her a glance. 'Can you understand that?'

Though he spoke lightly, there was something in his smile that made her guess suddenly at the pain he must have suffered the time she'd inadvertently let him down in the past.

He angled his lean, powerful frame a little further around to face her, leaning on his elbow, and said gently, 'See, Larissa, I want to know you're truly my family, my—wife. I don't want to ever risk losing you again.'

'Oh.' Her eyes were suddenly so misty everything became a beautiful blur. In fact, a few actual tears spilled over. With his usual courtesy, Alessandro helped her out by mopping her up with the corner of a beach towel, and making soothing noises.

She managed to reply at last. 'I think I *do* understand what you're saying. The marriage tradition is not completely unknown in Australia, you know. I wouldn't mind being put out of my single misery if the right man came along with a good offer.'

His brows went up. 'Oh? You wouldn't?' He searched her face with an intent, urgent gaze. 'Well, then… So… How about me? Will you marry me?'

Joy blazed in her heart in a fierce, pure flame that momentarily snatched away her ability to speak. He gazed silently at her, then she sat up and hugged him. 'Oh, my darling,' burst from her. 'Yes, and yes, and yes.' She accompanied each yes with a small passionate kiss.

He let out a long, shuddering breath. *'Grazie a Dio!'* His face lit with a smile and he seized her and held her close to him, stroking her hair. 'You won't be sorry, I promise. We'll be happy together because we love each other. Vivi will be happy. She'll be *safe*. I will take care of you both. Everyone will be happy. *Your* mother, *my* mother…' He broke into a wicked laugh. 'Wait until they meet at the wedding.'

'I can hardly imagine that.' She added nervously, 'The Meadowses don't really go in for grand splashes, you know.'

He grinned. 'No need to worry yourself about that, *tesoro*. The Vincentis will take care of everything. At your instruction, of course,' he added quickly. 'And we'll have to do something about the residence.'

She looked enquiringly at him. 'What residence?'

His thick black brows lifted. 'Our home. Do you have any ideas of where you'd like to live? I myself am used to seeing the sea wherever I live. Since childhood, you understand. Do you like ocean views?' She nodded, and he said, 'Good. We'll start looking when we get back to Sydney.'

She was just starting to consider the exciting residential possibilities when Alessandro's eyes lit with a piercing, sensual gleam.

'In the meantime, *tesoro*, maybe we can start thinking about our honeymoon.'

With the moon rising in the eastern sky, the surf lapping the beach and a balmy ocean breeze to fan their limbs, a lounger seemed an ideal place to contemplate some honeymoon possibilities. Alessandro's strong, warm arms slid around her, his sensuous lips embarked on a blissful exploration of her neck, and Lara gazed up into the tropical sky and, with all her heart, thanked the starlit heavens for all the treasures that were hers.

Bestselling Harlequin Presents author

Lynne Graham

brings you an exciting new miniseries:

PREGNANT BRIDES

Inexperienced and expecting, they're forced to marry

Collect them all:

DESERT PRINCE, BRIDE OF INNOCENCE
January 2010

RUTHLESS MAGNATE, CONVENIENT WIFE
February 2010

GREEK TYCOON, INEXPERIENCED MISTRESS
March 2010

TWO CROWNS, TWO ISLANDS, ONE LEGACY

A royal family torn apart by pride and its lust for power, reunited by purity and passion

Harlequin Presents is proud to bring you the final two installments from The Royal House of Karedes. As the stories unfold, secrets and sins from the past are revealed and desire, love and passion war with royal duty!

Look for:

RUTHLESS BOSS, ROYAL MISTRESS
by Natalie Anderson
January 2010

THE DESERT KING'S HOUSEKEEPER BRIDE
by Carol Marinelli
February 2010

HARLEQUIN *Presents* EXTRA

Presents Extra brings you
two new exciting collections!

MISTRESS BRIDES

*When temporary arrangements
become permanent!*

The Millionaire's Rebellious Mistress #85
by CATHERINE GEORGE

One Night In His Bed #86
by CHRISTINA HOLLIS

MEDITERRANEAN TYCOONS

At the ruthless tycoon's mercy

Kyriakis's Innocent Mistress #87
by DIANA HAMILTON

The Mediterranean's Wife by Contract #88
by KATHRYN ROSS

Available January 2010

REQUEST YOUR FREE BOOKS!

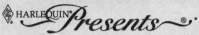 

2 FREE NOVELS
PLUS 2
FREE GIFTS!

HP09R

I ♥ HARLEQUIN® *Presents*

BROUGHT TO YOU BY FANS OF
HARLEQUIN PRESENTS.

We are its editors and authors
and biggest fans—and we'd
love to hear from YOU!

**Subscribe today to our online blog at
www.iheartpresents.com**